CATCH ME ONCE, CATCH ME TWICE

Also by Janet McNaughton:
To Dance at the Palais Royale

"Janet McNaughton provides a real plot, magic, adventure and thought-provoking characters."
— *CM (Canadian Materials)*

"McNaughton's Teen Tale a Winner. . .
This ia an audacious effort for a first chilren's novel. . . a tale well told, one that can transport today's childrent to a different era."
— *The Globe & Mail*

"Characterization is tight in this first novel. . . From the start, Ev promises to be a character whose adventrues will be worth following, and that promise is fulfilled. . . [Ev] is a character that readers will want to know more about."
— *Quill & Quire*

"This is a book young readers will throughly enjoy."
— *What's Happening*

"McNaughton. . . has a spendid time with her historical setting and the hint of fairy folk that still drifts over Newfoundland. . . the overall result is richly textured and satisfying."
— Pat Barclay, *Books in Canada*

For Melanie,
with best wishes,
Janet McNaughton

CATCH ME ONCE,
CATCH ME TWICE

JANET McNAUGHTON

*Stoddart Publishing gratefully acknowledges the support of
the Canada Council and the Ontario Arts Council in the
development of writing and publishing in Canada.*

Printed in 1996 by
Stoddart Publishing Co. Limited
34 Lesmill Road
Toronto, Canada
M3B 2T6
(416) 445-3333

First printed in 1994 by
Tuckamore Books a Creative Publishers imprint
P.O. Box 8660
St. John's Newfoundland
A1B 3T6

Canadian Cataloguing in Publication Data
McNaughton, Janet Elizabeth, 1953-
Catch me once, catch me twice

ISBN: 0-7736-1181-9
I. Title.
PS8575.N385C28   1996   jC813'.54   C96-930589-2
PZ7.M33Ca 1996

Cover design: Bill Douglas at The Bang
Cover illustration: Sharif Tarabay
Computer Graphics: Mary Bowness
Printed and bound in Canada

To my father, who was almost there in 1942,
and my mother, who always was, later.

Chapter One

"Late again, young lady!" As Ev entered the house, her grandmother's voice rang out from the dining room. Ev heard the annoyance in that voice, but underneath a kind of spiteful energy. Lateness gave her grandmother something to be angry about, and Ev was beginning to realize that her grandmother liked to be angry.

Ev hung up her old blue coat and straightened the always crooked sash on her school tunic. Then, before she could think too much about what she was doing, she reached into her pocket and took out a small jackknife. She slid the blade open quickly with her thumbnail and reached around into the closet, which had an elaborate wooden moulding on the doorframe, inside and out. Inside the closet, out of sight, she pushed her jackknife into the wood hard, gouging until a small piece of the varnished wood chipped onto the floor. There, she thought, be angry about that.

She snapped the knife shut, slipped it back into her pocket and took a deep breath, then went into the dining room as quickly as she could without running. "Ladies do not run," her grandmother liked to say, and would given half a chance.

Lady. Until she moved to St. John's two months ago no one had ever suggested Ev behave like one. She was happier roaming through the woods with her father than learning to knit or sew. Her father had been proud of her for that, often saying she was as good as a boy. And, although Ev had no desire to be a boy, she knew he'd intended it as a compliment.

The dining room table was set for noon dinner, with a white linen table cloth and the second-best china. Ev's grandmother sat alone at the head of the table. After Ev sat down and a quick grace was said, a bell was rung to tell Millie, the maid, to bring in the stew. Always beef stew for dinner on Tuesdays. While it was being served, Ev knew she would receive her daily lecture on lateness.

Maybe I can distract her, she thought, and taking a deep breath she asked, "Where is Mum, Grandmother? Is she sick?"

"Indisposed is a much better word Evelyn. Your speech is so common. But I suppose that is to be expected with you growing up in outports." She sighed her disapproval. Ev's grandmother had moved to Newfoundland from Canada almost forty years before, but never really adapted to being here. "Yes, your mother is indisposed today and I do not think you should bother her. Heartburn, she said, which is to be expected in her condition."

Her condition. Ev's grandmother would never even say "expecting a baby." She seemed to think the word pregnant was indecent. She acts as if she's ashamed that Mum is having a baby, Ev thought.

Then Ev remembered. How could she have forgotten, even for a moment? "Any mail today?" She tried to keep her voice calm and even.

Ev's grandmother looked at her more kindly now. She knew why Ev was asking. "Yes, there was, and no, there wasn't anything from your father."

They hadn't heard from Ev's father in weeks. Not since his first letter from North Africa. Why doesn't he write? she thought. What if he's not okay?

"You mustn't be discouraged Evelyn," her grandmother said. "If anything was wrong we'd be told. I'm sure your father wouldn't want us to spend time worrying when we can contribute to the war effort instead." This was her grandmother's stiff upper lip speech. Ev heard it at least once a week. It was as close to sympathy as she ever came.

I'll worry about my father if I want to, Ev thought. If only Dad hadn't gone to fight the Nazis. Then we wouldn't be living here with Grandmother and Grandpa. We'd be back in Trinity Bay in our own house and everything would be just like it used to.

Millie brought dinner in. She was an outport

girl, unaccustomed to St. John's ways and Evelyn's stern grandmother. Now, she nervously spilled a little of the gravy from a plate on to the tablecloth. Ev saw before her grandmother did. She considered distracting her grandmother to save Millie from trouble, but decided to say nothing. Let Grandmother be angry with someone else for a change, she thought. At least Millie gets paid for putting up with her.

Ev's grandmother had sharp eyes. She noticed almost right away. "Mildred, see what you've done! Clumsy girl."

"Yes Missus, sorry Missus," Millie said, turning red. She was only seventeen and already earning a living far from her home. But it was too late for Ev to be sorry, for Millie disappeared into the kitchen and Ev's grandmother turned to her. "Your Grandfather isn't able to join us today. He's at the hospital. One of his patients broke an arm."

Too bad, Ev thought. Dinner wouldn't be so dull if Grandpa were home.

As Ev ate, she studied the dining room. Sunlight poured in through lace curtains. Crystals in the chandelier caught the sun, casting rainbows onto the yellow plaster above the dark wood panelling. Sunshine was rare in November. This was a beautiful room and even the heavy blackout curtains, now drawn back to let in the light, could not make it gloomy today. Ev sighed. Living in this big house in a city like St. John's could have been an adventure. Instead, it seemed more like a trial.

While they ate, Ev's grandmother questioned her about the morning's school work. Ev answered as briefly as she could. The sound of her grandmother's voice grated on her ears today, reminding Ev of the conversation she had overheard the night before. Ev hadn't meant to eavesdrop. She came out of the bathroom intending to go straight upstairs to her room when the sound of her own name drifted up from the hall below. Her grandmother was on the telephone.

"No, Evelyn isn't fitting in at all," the floating voice had said, "But I hardly wonder. Duncan and Nina have spoiled the child, that's plain to see. She's so headstrong and stubborn. Of course, Duncan was rather like that at her age, but it's unbecoming in a girl, don't you think? And I do wish she'd take more care with her appearance. That hair! If only she could find a way to keep it pinned back properly. I wish she was more like your Letty..."

For a few seconds, Ev felt as if her grandmother's words had frozen her in place. Then she turned and fled up the stairs to the shelter of her own room, not waiting to hear the rest. She had never heard anyone talk like that about her. Of course she was like her father. Even the thick, dark and curly hair her grandmother found so objectionable came from him. At first, Ev had expected her grandmother to love her because she was so much like her father. After all, her father was an only child, and Ev was the only grandchild, at least until the new baby came. But everything about Ev seemed to displease her grandmother. Now she barely hoped to be liked by her.

It was a relief to leave the table when dinner was over. Ev went straight to the bookshelf in the parlour. After her father went overseas in the fall, she had started to read all the books she could find in her grandparents' house that had her father's name, Duncan McCallum, written in his fine, firm handwriting on the flyleaf. Sometimes just running her fingers over his signature could make her feel better. She was a fast reader and quickly finished all the adventure books from his boyhood. She especially like *Kidnapped* by Robert Louis Stevenson.

Only the more difficult books remained now, but Ev found she could not stop. Somehow, without realizing it, she had decided that reading these books was important to her father's safety. If she stopped, something terrible would happen to him. When her grandparents noticed her reading, they only smiled in approval. No one suspected how important this was, how vital to her father's welfare. And this was why she was now making her way, with difficulty, through *A Midsummer-Night's Dream* by William Shakespeare.

It wasn't as bad as she'd expected. Some of the words were difficult to understand, and she didn't care for the four mindless lovers, stumbling around in the woods like fools, but she liked the bumbling tradesmen who were trying to put off a play, and most of all she liked the fairies. They reminded her of the fairies that were supposed to be out on the barrens near her home in Belbin's Cove. Not pretty, harmless things, but creatures with the power to do good or evil as they saw fit.

Just now, where she was reading, the fairy king and queen were arguing over a little boy they both wanted. Ev enjoyed the queen's description of ships at sea, how the sails grew "big-bellied with the wanton wind." It reminded her of the old schooners she sometimes saw out on Trinity Bay from Belbin's Cove. Then the queen spoke of the mother of the little boy they were fighting over, how she had looked like a ship at sea when she was expecting her baby, reminding Ev of her own mother.

But then the queen said of the child's mother, "but she, being mortal, of that boy did die." Ev snapped the book shut. It was as if it had bitten her. No one spoke about it, but they were all afraid something like that would happen to her mother. She knew. She slipped her hand into the pocket of her tunic and cradled the jackknife in her palm. The weight of it, the coolness, calmed her.

Now Ev had to see her mother. There was just time enough to steal upstairs before returning to school. She's my mother, Ev thought, no one can tell me when I can and can't see her. Ev climbed the carpeted stairs to the third floor without a sound and stood outside the bedroom that was now her mother's, peeking through the half open door. The form on the bed was so still that her mother seemed to be sleeping. The new baby was due in only a few weeks, and even from the back Ev could see how it shaped her mother's body. Then she heard a sniffle. Her mother was crying again. Oh, great, Ev thought. Go ahead and cry.

No one expects you to do anything else, do they? Ev went downstairs, this time not caring if anyone heard her or not. It was time to go back to school anyway. She put on her coat and left the house without saying goodbye to anyone.

There was a time when Ev had never heard her mother cry. It was hard to believe that was less than a year ago. But her mother began to cry when her father announced that he was going off to fight, and cried often since they came to live with her father's parents in September. Her mother said she always cried easily when she was carrying Ev, that there must be something about expecting a child that did this to her. Ev wasn't frightened by her mother's tears any more, but she wished her mother would show some backbone. She acts like a child, Ev thought. You'd never guess she came to Newfoundland from England all by herself and worked alone in outport nursing stations before she married Dad. It's mostly Grandmother's fault, the way she is now, Ev thought. All Grandmother needs is standing up to. But somehow Ev's mother never could.

Out in the sunshine, under the pale blue sky, it was easy, just for a moment, to forget the war and all her troubles. No snow had fallen yet, the walk from her grandparents' house to school went quickly. This walk was one of the few things about St. John's that Ev had learned to love in the past two months. She could look down to the harbour and even out to sea for much of the way. The war had made the ocean a dangerous place, but the harbour itself was safe. It was almost like a lake, completely surrounded by land except for the small opening to the sea called the Narrows. On either side of that opening, wild looking, high hills hugged St. John's like great rock arms. After the war began, a submarine net was strung across the Narrows to make the harbour even more secure. Once, last year, her grandfather told her, this net was torpedoed by an unseen German submarine. The torpedo had not exploded, but even now Ev shuddered to think of the enemy so near.

Just a few weeks ago, the *Caribou*, the ferry that carried passengers between Newfoundland and Cape Breton, was torpedoed and sank. Many lives were lost; not only men, but women and children too. Sometimes it seemed to Ev as if that submarine net was the only thing that stood between St. John's and the war.

Now, so much smoke was rising from the funnels of ships in the harbour below that Ev guessed a convoy was forming. The boats would gather without anyone knowing when the ships would leave or where they were bound, then two huge winches, one on either side of the Narrows, would lower the submarine net to let them pass. Ev's classroom had a fine view of the harbour and her teacher found it difficult to make the boys concentrate on their studies on those days when there were convoys to be seen.

St. John's sloped towards the harbour like a great bowl with uneven sides. By Ev's school there was a sharp drop, almost a cliff beside the road. The school was built against this, and Ev could enter the third floor here, but the playground and the first floor were far below. Down there, other children crowded the schoolyard now, playing noisy games or standing in small groups. Ev had made some friends, but today it felt better to be alone up here, leaning on the wrought iron fence beside the top floor of the school, looking out at the smoke from the ships in the harbour and waiting to see if the submarine net would be lowered soon.

While she watched, her problems crowded back into her mind. Why is Grandmother so hard on Mum? she wondered. It seemed that her grandmother somehow blamed her mother for the coming baby. Ev had always wanted a brother or sister, but there had been a number of mishaps, she knew, when her mother had not been able to carry a baby until it could be born. Then she could remember her parents telling her not to wish for a brother or a sister because there wouldn't be one. It was a little lonely, but Ev never really minded. She was happy, helping her mother in the garden, going trouting with her father in the summer. Ev had never doubted that she was the most important person in the world to them.

Then the war came. It seemed so far away at first, and even though gasoline was rationed and some food was scarce, it was easy to believe the war would never touch them. But her father had taken it all so seriously, sitting beside the big floor radio in their parlour each night listening to the BBC news, reading the newspapers over and over. Ev and her mother never suspected that he would decide to join up. Married men hardly ever did. Her father seemed easy going, but underneath he had a stubborn streak, and when he announced his decision to enlist, late last winter, nothing anyone could say would change his mind.

Ev's mother argued at first, then cried. Then something else happened. Ev woke up one night to the sound of her mother in tears and she heard her father say gently, "Nina, if you thought this would change my mind, you were mistaken. I'm as determined as ever to go. This is a terrible risk you're taking, but it can't be undone."

Ev fell back into a troubled sleep. A few days later her parents announced that she and her mother would move into St. John's to live with her father's parents when he went overseas. Until now, Ev had only seen her grandparents at Christmas, and she was always glad when it was time to leave their stuffy home. She couldn't believe her parents would do this to her. It seemed as if they were trying to take everything away.

"I don't want to leave here," she cried, "It's not fair. Nobody said anything about this before. Why should we go to town?"

"You'll like living in town, Ev," her mother said, "You'll go to one of the best schools, the one your father went to. And think of the stores. We won't have to order your clothes by mail any more. As soon as the weather gets cool, we'll go down to Water Street and pick out a new winter coat. Any one you want."

"There's nothing wrong with my old coat," Ev said. You can't buy me, she thought.

Her parents looked uncomfortable. Then her father spoke. "You'll both be better off with someone to look out for you. Your mother will be needing a doctor and your grandfather is the best one I know."

"What are you talking about? Is Mum sick?" This was getting worse and worse.

There was another embarrassed pause and then her mother said, "You know that little brother or sister you've always wanted Ev? Well perhaps now you'll have one." And that was how they told Ev about the baby. No one had looked very happy.

As summer passed, Ev refused to talk about moving to town. Surely something would happen to keep her father from going. Maybe the war would end. She left the room whenever her parents mentioned St. John's. She let her parents do all the packing.

The harsh clang of the school bell cut into Ev's thoughts. Below her, everyone began to file into the school. But when Ev reached the door marked "Girls" on the third floor, it was locked. This door was never locked. Should she try the nearby Boys' entrance, or go down to the playground below? She kicked the door in frustration, hurting her toes, then turned and hurried around to the steep steps on the side of the hill leading down to the schoolyard.

As she rounded the corner to the schoolyard, she saw a group of bigger boys who had lagged behind make their way towards the Boys' door. She didn't know most of them, but she recognized Peter Tilley who was in her class although he was fourteen. Peter had lost two years of school because of an infection in his leg. He seemed well now, but was left with a painful-looking limp, and he often used a cane. As he made his way into school, one of the boys Ev knew as a bully held out his foot and tripped Peter so that he fell to the ground. The other boys laughed. One said, "Cripple!" and another, "Nanny's boy." They began to walk away.

Ev watched Peter reach for his cane, then slip it neatly between the feet of the boy who had tripped him. He came down heavily with a cry of surprise while Peter rose to his feet. The two boys squared off, red faced and panting, and Ev thought there was sure to be a fight. Peter was taller, but the other boy had a heavier build. It was easy to see who would win, but Peter showed no sign of backing down.

Just then, a teacher stepped out from one of the doors. "Come along, all of you," she said shortly and the confrontation was over. Ev rushed into the school, up the stairs and into her classroom.

Miss Smith, her teacher, finished addressing the class before she looked at Ev. ". . . and if the person who blocked up the girls' entrance from Harvey Road is apprehended, the punishment will be severe. Pranks of this sort will not be tolerated." Then she turned to Ev, "Late again, Evelyn. You must learn to arrive on time, dear.

This isn't some little outport school, you know."

Although she hadn't meant to be unkind, Miss Smith's words brought sniggers of laughter from some of Ev's classmates, who looked down on people "from around the bay." Thanks a lot, Ev thought and she threw herself into her seat without looking at anyone. When Peter arrived even later, Miss Smith was not so kind. "You'll never catch up on your work, Peter Tilley, if you come in late like this. Next time you'll be sent to the headmistress."

How stupid can you get, Ev thought. It's hardly Peter's fault he's late. "But Miss Smith . . ." she began. Suddenly, everyone in the class was looking at her. Ev stopped. Then Peter caught her eye. He gave her a look that was something like an annoyed plea, and Ev realized that speaking up for him wouldn't help.

"Yes, Evelyn?" The teacher waited for her to say something.

"Nothing Miss Smith, sorry," she said.

The afternoon dragged on until it was finally time to go home. By now, the sun was gone behind a featureless blanket of grey clouds and fog had rolled in off the sea. Two girls from Ev's class, Letitia Winsor and Doris Piercy, waited for her. They both came from what Ev's grandmother called "good families," meaning, as far as Ev could tell, that their fathers made a lot of money. Ev knew them mainly because their grandmothers were friends of Ev's grandmother. On Saturdays, the three girls worked at the Women's Patriotic Association together, packing wool for women in outports who were knitting for servicemen. Ev knew she was supposed to feel grateful to Letty and Doris for their friendship. Somehow, she never did.

Letty was a tiny girl who wore her blonde hair in fat sausage curls that she claimed were natural. This was the girl Ev's grandmother wanted her to be. Letty seemed to think of herself as pretty, though she looked thin and pinched to Ev. Doris was tall, like Ev. Of the two, she seemed nicer, but she always did exactly what Letty wanted. Today, the two girls were talking excitedly about the latest movie at the Nickel, the theatre they passed on the way home.

"It's called 'Mrs. Miniver'," Letty said. "With Greer Garson."

"Oh, she's some pretty," said Doris.

Letty gave Doris a cold look. "Doris," she said. "Only maids and baymen say 'some pretty'."

Doris looked hurt, but said nothing.

"Anyway," Letty continued, "You should see it, Ev. It's about a woman who keeps the home fires burning during the war, just like your Mom."

That didn't sound anything like Ev's mother, but she nodded anyway. She would rather die than tell these girls what a sook her mother had become.

Letty and Doris were always talking about the movies. Ev knew they saw her own situation as a sort of movie come to life, and that was one reason they were friendly with her. And maybe it sounded glamorous to have a father fighting in the war and a mother expecting a baby, but it didn't feel much like a Hollywood movie. Other than movies, Letty and Doris only wanted to talk about clothes and boys. All this should have made them seem older than the children Ev grew up with, but somehow it didn't. Ev's friends at home all had their work to do. Boys fished with their fathers like men in the summer and the girls knew how to bake bread, knit mittens and care for younger children. They made pampered "townies" like Doris and Letty seem like small children.

"You're some quiet today, Ev," Doris said after a while. "I mean, you're awfully quiet," she quickly corrected herself.

"Ev thinks she's too good for us," Letty said, "Because she's the only one who has a father overseas."

"No I don't," Ev said. Well, maybe she did, but she wasn't going to come right out and say it.

"You do so. I've seen the way you look at us sometimes."

It was true that Ev wasn't sure she wanted to be friends with Letty and Doris. Did that mean she was stuck up?

"I don't think I'm better than you," Ev said. She hoped she sounded as if she meant it.

"Then prove it," Letty said.

"How?"

"Well..." Letty was thinking. In spite of the coolness of the day, Ev's palms began to sweat.

"I know," Letty said finally, "If you're really

our friend, you'll do anything I dare you to."

By now, they had reached the corner near Ev's grandparents' house. The three girls paused on the sidewalk. Ev had never refused a dare. In Belbin's Cove she'd balanced on barrels of cod liver oil and walked the edge of the hydro dam on First Pond that her father helped to build. "All right," she said now. "I'm not afraid." She wasn't either. This would be easy.

"Okay," said Letty. "I dare you to put my lipstick on and kiss a boy." Letty wasn't allowed to wear makeup but she kept a lipstick hidden in her desk.

"What boy?" Doris said. She giggled. "Jack Miller?" Jack was a plump, good-natured boy who didn't mind a joke. Ev realized that Doris was trying to be kind.

But Letty brushed the suggestion aside. "Peter Tilley," she said.

Ev felt her stomach knot, but she wasn't surprised. Most of the boys in their class seemed like babies. Peter was the oldest, and he was good-looking. Ev knew Letty secretly wished he'd notice her, even though she said she'd never go out with someone like Peter who was just a fisherman's son. This wasn't like any dare Ev had ever had before, but she didn't know how to get out of it.

Letty saw her hesitate. "What's the matter Ev? You scared?"

That did it. "No, I'm not scared," Ev almost shouted.

"Then will you do it?"

"Of course I will." The words were out before Ev could stop herself.

"Good. We'll see you tomorrow," Letty said. She walked away with Doris, both of them chattering and giggling.

Some friends.

Chapter Two

Ev headed straight for the big, bright kitchen when she came into her grandparents' house. Millie often had a pot of tea on the stove. How could I let Letty trick me like this? she thought. Luckily, Tuesday was one of her grandmother's war effort afternoons. There would be time to think without having to be polite.

But Ev stopped short when she reached the kitchen door. There, at the table, where Ev herself usually sat was the strangest looking creature, a little old woman all dressed in black, with bright, bird-like eyes, her tiny hands curled around her teacup.

"Come right in, my dear," she said to Ev in a piping voice, as if this were her own kitchen. For just a moment, Ev wondered if she was in the wrong house. "You'd be young Evelyn, I imagine. I've just had the nicest kind of chat with your mother, and she told me all about you." Ev hesitated, wondering who on earth this woman might be. Her clothes were clean, but worn and out of fashion. This was certainly no friend of her grandmother's.

"Come in, come in," the old woman repeated. "No need to be shy, my dear. I'm just having a drop of tea till my grandson comes for me. Millie left the pot on the stove for you. She's just up seeing to your mother. Pour yourself a cup and sit down."

Ev did as she was told, looking for a way to ask this woman who she was. But before she could even sit down, her grandfather joined them. She could never recall her grandfather visiting the kitchen before. With his tweed suit and carefully brushed silver hair, he seemed out of place among the pots and dishes. Even more surprising was the way he addressed the stranger.

"Oh, hello Evelyn. Well, Mrs. Bursey, you've seen Nina. What's your opinion?"

The old lady gave a cautious glance in Ev's direction before speaking, but a nod from Ev's grandfather told her she could be frank. Ev breathed a silent sigh of relief. She would hate to be sent from the room like a small child. "Well now, doctor, 'tis only natural that she should long for her husband at a time like this, and the worry is putting a great strain on her and the baby. But 'tis a problem of the heart, not the body, and the child seems as right as can be. What do you think?"

Ev was amazed. Her grandfather and this old woman were talking like equals. "I think you're right," he said. "I just wanted someone to confirm my own opinion, and I knew of no one better than you." Then he turned to Ev. "I've asked Mrs. Bursey to visit your mother from time to time. Sarah Bursey's the best midwife in St. John's. If she thinks things are going well, we can all relax."

"Now then, doctor," Mrs. Bursey said, obviously pleased, "Don't go turning an old woman's head with your flattery."

"We'll see about getting you home now," Dr. McCallum said.

"No need. My grandson will be here any moment to help me home. I asked him to call for me at four-thirty."

"Nonsense. I won't hear of you walking home, grandson or no. I'll drive you both."

Just then, there was a knock at the kitchen door.

"Four-thirty," observed Mrs. Bursey, "Set your watch by that youngster."

When Ev opened the door there was Peter Tilley. "What are you doing here?" she blurted out. Could he somehow have found out about the dare?

"I've come for my Nan," he said. He looked embarrassed. Neither of them moved.

"Evelyn, for heaven's sake, don't keep Peter standing "outside." Her grandfather's good-natured exasperation made it possible for Ev to move, and Peter entered the kitchen.

Ev couldn't even look at Peter, so she turned to her grandfather instead. "I'm sorry Grandpa," she said, "I was surprised. You see, Peter is in my class at school and for a moment I couldn't think what he was doing here."

Her grandfather seemed pleased. "So you know each other? Good. Peter, you should come around some time. Ev still hasn't made many friends."

Not only that, Ev thought, I'm probably about to lose the only two I have.

"Ev's a great one for fishing," her grandfather continued, "Too bad it's so late in the season."

Peter looked at her in disbelief. "Fishing?" he asked.

Ev's grandfather, who knew nothing about the outdoors, had used the wrong word. Ev knew that Peter was trying to picture her hauling nets or jigging for cod on the ocean.

"No, Grandpa, trouting," she corrected.

"Oh, there's a difference, is there?" Her grandfather laughed "You see, Mrs. Bursey, I'm still a foreigner after all these years."

But Mrs. Bursey spoke to Evelyn. "Well, my child, we lives right by the water, out to the Battery." Ev was surprised. She could see the Battery from her bedroom window and often looked at the little houses out by the Narrows, but never suspected any of her classmates lived there. "If you should want to go fishing," Mrs. Bursey continued, "Peter's the lad. Has his own boat and he's still a fine hand on the water, even with his leg gone bad and all." She spoke of Peter's handicap without embarrassment.

"Boat's hauled up for the season now," Peter

said. His words were short, but there was nothing surly in his tone. In fact, Ev noticed a certain liveliness had crept into his usually cautious manner as soon as fishing was mentioned.

"Well, it's almost blackout time. I'll drive you both home," Dr. McCallum said. "I'll just fetch my overcoat." Then, turning to Ev he added, "Why don't you visit with your mother for a while? Take her up a cup of that tea."

I suppose I might as well, Ev thought, and as Mrs. Bursey and Peter left with her grandfather, she poured a cup of tea for her mother. Peter was shy, but he seemed nicer than Doris or Letty, more like her friends back in Belbin's Cove. At least he was interested in something besides movies and clothes.

Ev passed Millie on the stairs and went into her mother's room. Nina McCallum was small, blonde and fragile with soft brown eyes. Not at all like Ev. She was sitting up in bed now, looking quite cheerful for once.

"How are you Mum?" Ev asked. This was the way things went now. Once, Ev would have been happy to tell her mother all about the trouble Letty was causing. Now she knew she shouldn't bother her.

"I'm just fine Ev. My, what a proper old dear that Mrs. Bursey is. Such a gentle, kindly touch. You know, I feel better than I have for days. Look," her mother continued. "She brought me some pattern books for baby sweaters. Aren't they lovely? Help me pick out a pattern Ev." And Ev knelt on her mother's bed, her own dark head close to her mother's fair one, studying the patterns until Millie came to tell them it was time for supper.

"I think I feel well enough to come down for supper tonight," Ev's mother said, lifting herself off the bed. As Ev followed her mother downstairs, she silently thanked Mrs. Bursey.

By now, the blackout curtains were pulled across the dining room windows. No enemy aircraft had passed near Newfoundland, but they might, and the blackout was seen as a necessary precaution. But Ev hated black and she hated those curtains. They made her think of funerals. In the back of her mind, she always wondered who had died.

Supper at the McCallum household was formal compared to the relaxed meals Ev had been accustomed to at home, although the food was not as good as it had been before the war. But tonight her grandfather seemed more lively than usual. Maybe it's because he's not so worried about Mum, Ev thought. Even Ev's mother stayed cheerful, and her grandmother seemed content to tell the stories she'd heard during her afternoon at the WPA, knitting for soldiers overseas.

"Really, Ian," she said with spirit, "It's almost embarrassing to be a Canadian under these circumstances. The Canadian servicemen are the really wild ones if the stories are to be believed, far worse than the Americans. Wandering around drunk, taking cars for joy riding, accosting young women. . ." she began, then glanced at Ev and thought better. "Can't you do something?"

"Me? What am I to do, Gwen?"

"Well, some of them must be Presbyterian. Perhaps you could speak to the commanding officers, get the men into church on Sundays."

"Put the fear of God into them, is that it?" Ev's grandfather laughed. "It may be too late for that." Even Ev's mother laughed with him.

When supper was finished, Millie took the plates away and brought in a fresh pot of tea and a blueberry pie made with berries Ev had picked with her father near Belbin's Cove in August. Ev's mother took the pie from Millie and began to cut it into slices with an energy that reminded Ev of the days before all their troubles began. Maybe now, Ev thought, she'll be more like she used to be.

Then Ev's grandmother spoke. "Nina, those pieces are far too big. There is a war on, you know. You'd better let me do that."

It was a little thing, really, but Ev could see her mother crumple as she silently passed the pie over. She hardly touched her piece. I'll make you pay for hurting my mother, Ev thought. Ev's grandfather noticed too. "Heartburn again Nina?" he asked. Ev's mother nodded. He smiled at her. "Well, you know what the old midwives say. That means your baby will have lots of hair. Now I don't know if that's true, but Gwen always had heartburn when she was carrying Duncan, and he had masses of curls, didn't he Gwen?"

For once, Ev's grandmother was at a loss for words. "Really, Ian," she finally sputtered, "How can you talk like that in front of Evelyn?"

Ev had to pinch herself to keep from laughing.

"Well, you can't expect Ev to go on believing that the stork brings babies. Not with all this evidence to the contrary." He winked at Ev across the table. But Ev's mother didn't even smile. She remained silent and left the table as soon as she could.

After supper, Ev took her father's copy of *A Midsummer-Night's Dream* from the parlour and went upstairs. She could hear her grandparents talking in the dining room. As she passed their bedroom on the second floor, she paused. Her grandmother's silver dresser set and perfumes were neatly laid out on her vanity table, a useless-looking affair with a big round mirror and a few small drawers. Ev knew her grandmother was especially fond of this table. She quickly glanced around to see that no one was near. No one was. Millie was doing the dishes, her grandparents were in the parlour and her mother was already in her bedroom above.

Ev felt for the knife in her pocket. She hesitated, but only for a moment. Then she quickly slipped inside the bedroom and studied the legs of the vanity while she took out the knife. There were some small, ornamental bits of wood at the bottom of the legs. Ev slipped her knife into the space where one of these was joined. She only meant to nick it, but the piece was glued, not nailed and it pried off neatly, splitting the wood at the bottom where the glue held. Ev looked at her handiwork in horror, then she stuck the piece back in place and ran upstairs. Perhaps no one would notice. Across the hall from Ev's room, tiny, muffled sobs came from behind her mother's door. They cut into Ev's heart like a knife. Just for that moment, her anger gave way to something else, a feeling so black it didn't even have a name. But she quickly pushed the feeling aside. You won't help me, she said silently to her mother, so I can't help you.

Ev went into her own room and closed the door. Anyway, she thought, I have my work to do. I have to read Dad's book. But it was hard to concentrate tonight. She kept thinking of Letty Winsor. This is what a mouse must feel like when a cat has it, Ev thought. She knew that Letty imagined she could play with her like this for as long as she wanted to. Just thinking about it gave her a headache. After a while, Ev was glad to go back to Shakespeare.

Later, just before she went to sleep, Ev took the knife from the pocket of her school tunic and held it in her hand, remembering one evening last August in Belbin's Cove. It had been a bad day. Ev's mother told her that most of her books were to be packed away and left in the house. It was too expensive, she said, to ship them down to St. John's. Ev protested to her father, but he only said, "There's no shortage of books in St. John's." How could he not understand that every one of those books was like an old friend?

After supper, when Ev's mother tried to measure her for her school tunics, Ev refused. "You can't make me and I won't," she cried. "I'll hate those tunics and I'll hate that school and. . . and I hate you." Ev had never said that before. The words seemed to echo in the shocked silence that followed. The worst thing was that her mother didn't even try to fight back. She just stood there with the tape measure in her hand, tears spilling from her mild brown eyes, making Ev hate herself without saying a word. Ev turned and ran from the house as fast as she could, taking the road towards the cove.

The sun had already disappeared over the ridge on the western side of Belbin's Cove. Along the road, dragonflies hummed and darted after mosquitos. When she reached the cove, the water was dead calm, and women were still gathering armloads of salt fish off the flakes for the night. Their friendly voices carried over the water. High above, some small clouds turned bright pink, reflecting a sunset Ev could not see. The breeze ruffled her dress around her bare legs.

It made Ev ache to think she couldn't stay here. She closed her eyes, held her breath and wished as hard as she could. Let me be a rock, a wooden longer in the flakes, a wave on the land-wash, she thought, anything, just so I never, ever have to leave this place. But when she opened her eyes, nothing had changed. Well, Ev thought, only babies believe in magic. She stood alone on the slipway for a long time, hugging her arms tight. When she heard the crunch of boots on the road behind her, she didn't bother to look around. She knew her father's footfall. He sat on a boulder near the slipway not speaking. Ev could not look at him. Finally he spoke, keeping his voice low, so that only she could hear him.

"There's a terrible evil over there," he said. "At first I thought, this is just another war. But it isn't. You can't expect me to sit here and let others fight for me." Ev thought he would be mad, but this was worse, a tiredness in his voice she had never heard before. Finally she turned to look at him.

"There's room on this rock for two," he said. Ev came and sat beside him while he continued. "I know you're finding it difficult to accept the changes," he said. "More than I thought you would. Of course, I never imagined you'd have to leave here. The baby was, well, unexpected. I'm not sure how you'll get along with my parents. The truth is, they think we've spoiled you. In these last few weeks, I've wondered if they aren't right.

"You see, my parents were so strict with me, when I realized you were going to be an only child too, I didn't want to make the same mistakes. You're used to getting what you want, and I think that's good. But now you have to realize there's more to life than that. There's a war on Ev, and you're not a little child any more. You're twelve now. We're all making sacrifices. I'm giving up a few years of my life, and you've got to do your part as well.

"I'm worried about your mother. These temper tantrums of yours have got to stop. If you keep acting like this after I'm gone, I can't see how she will cope. Ev, you're much stronger than she is. I want you to promise me, when you go to town, that you won't make trouble for your mother and you won't fight with your grandparents. This is very important Ev."

He paused. He almost never asked her to promise anything, and she had never refused.

"Can you do that for me?" he asked.

Ev hesitated. Even if some people thought she was spoiled, she always kept a promise, no matter how difficult it seemed. In return, her parents never lied to her, and always kept their promises. That was an important part of what made them a family, different from other families Ev knew.

"You promise?" Her father drove a hard bargain.

Ev sighed. He'd be gone in a few weeks. How could she say no? "Cross my heart, hope to die," she said, tracing an X on her chest while she spoke. Now Ev knew he was really going and nothing she could say would stop him. Don't cry, don't cry you sissy, she told herself, but the tears came anyway.

Her father pretended not to notice, but he reached into his pocket and put something into her hand. "Here, I've been meaning to give this to you. It was mine when I was a kid."

It was the knife Ev held now, a knife with a white bone handle and a small steel blade. "If I have time before I go, I'll show you how to use it," he said.

There hadn't been time. But Ev made the promise and she tried to keep it. After that, Ev helped with the packing, stopped fighting with her mother, and now, she was always polite to her grandparents. She never made trouble for anyone. Her father had taken the promise from her. But he left the knife.

Ev slipped it under her pillow and turned off the light. There was no noise from her mother's room and Ev hoped she was asleep. But before she tried to sleep herself, she silently asked her mother the thing she wished but could never bring herself to say.

"Please, Mum," she thought, "Couldn't you be the grownup again?"

When Ev woke the next morning a bad feeling hung over her like a dark cloud. What was it? Then she remembered. Letty and her lipstick. She rose from her warm bed reluctantly. During breakfast and on the way to school she wondered if Letty might back down. Maybe she wasn't as mean as she seemed. Maybe it was just a joke. But she knew as soon as she walked into the schoolyard that Letty would not let her forget. She was there, standing with Doris, smirking. "At recess," she said, and then the bell rang. That was all, but Ev knew what she meant.

At recess, Ev went to the girls' washroom, hoping Letty would wait for her in the school-yard. Maybe I can stay here all recess, she thought. But when she walked out of the stall, Letty was there. A small crowd of girls gathered around as Ev washed her hands. They all seemed to know what was happening. Letty Winsor smiled and held out the lipstick. The cylinder of mock gold gleamed in her hand.

"Come on, Ev," she said, "You're not going to back down now, are you?"

Ev wished with all her heart that she was back in Belbin's Cove. Nothing like this would happen to her there. She reached out and took the lipstick. It felt cool and smooth and hard. I could do it, she thought. And then what? Would Letty like me any better? It would certainly end any hope of friendship with Peter. Ev took a deep breath.

"Letty," she said, "If you want to see Peter Tilley kissed so badly, kiss him yourself." She thrust the lipstick back into Letty's hand. Some of the girls giggled. Letty's eyes widened in surprise. Ev turned and ran outside.

Ev managed to avoid Letty and Doris for the rest of the day, but after school they waited for her. Letty still looked mad. She didn't waste any time.

"Evelyn McCallum, that was a nasty thing you did to me today, making me look like a fool in front of all those girls. You apologize."

Ev looked at Letty. She wasn't anyone Ev would have chosen for a friend at home. She knew if she apologized, it would only be a question of waiting until Letty thought of some other reason to quarrel. "Letty, I'm not sorry," Ev said, "You asked for it." Her voice was calm but her heart pounded in her ears.

Past Letty, Ev saw Doris's mouth drop open. Nobody spoke to Letty Winsor that way. Letty turned red, then spun on her heel and walked away.

"Come on, Doris," she said, "We know when we're not wanted."

Doris followed with only a brief backward glance.

Ev sighed. It was hard to lose the only friends she'd made since she came to St. John's, even if they weren't very good friends.

Chapter Three

"Well, my dear, I told her, your nipples will get some sore if you don't hold that youngster properly while you nurses her, and didn't she get an abscessed breast. Youngsters! Can't tell them nothing at all these days! Shocking is what it is, Mrs. Bursey."

The woman's voice carried upstairs to Peter's bedroom. There was no way to ignore it. After supper, especially on Fridays, the small house he shared with his Nan was too often filled with women talking about things he didn't or wasn't supposed to understand: pregnancy, breast feeding, colic in babies, female complaints. It was enough to put a fellow off women altogether. When his father had lived here, the women hadn't been around all the time like this. Now that they were, Peter usually escaped to his father's fishing store, the place where the nets and gear had always been kept. He took his jacket now and went outside to the shed across the road, built half on a rock outcrop and half on pilings high above the water. Here he could hear the waves lapping under him and feel close to the sea. There was a lamp and he'd rigged some old blinds to cover the windows so he could read when he wanted, but tonight Peter just sat in the dark, looking out over the water and thinking.

In this part of St. John's called the Battery, small frame houses were scattered over steep rock outcrop in a thinning line that reached towards the Narrows. Above and behind them towered Signal Hill, a landmark that was visible from most of the city. Canadian and American troops were stationed there now. At the foot of the Battery, the harbour stretched out and Peter could look back to the rest of St. John's, or off through the Narrows to the endless ocean.

There wasn't much in the way of gear in this old store now; Peter's father sold off most of it before heading out to work at the American naval base in Argentia. No point in saving it for Peter, he'd said offhandedly, he'd never make a fisherman now, not with that leg, and Peter had agreed, trying not to think of the emptiness he felt in his gut as he watched all those good nets and traps and hand lines go. The worst of it was the selling of his father's trap skiff, a sound white boat with red gunwales. The very first memory Peter had was of being handed down off the wharf by some unknown man over those gunwales into the arms of his father. He might have been two or three, and he'd crowed with delight to finally be allowed in the big, sturdy skiff.

Well, his father said he was finished fishing. "No money in it, boy," he'd said. "It's a whole new world out there now. Newfoundland will never be the same." At least he hadn't suggested they sell Peter's own small boat. His father made good money now working for the American military, money that helped support Peter and his Nan, and pay Peter's school fees and the doctors bills still left from his illness. Argentia seemed to suit Peter's father. He never came home on weekends as other men did. Peter wondered if he needed his freedom that much, after living with a small boy and an old woman all these years, that he had to disappear just as Peter began to need him around. He could at least write, but he never did. Peter missed his father, but he could not forgive him for turning away from the sea. Maybe that was why he never came home.

The store itself was like a ghost of the place it had once been when his father and the other men sat here in winter, mending their gear and telling stories, playing pranks, smoking. From the time he could walk, this was where Peter wanted to be. There were other places nearby now where the men still met, places Peter would be welcome. He knew his Nan imagined that was where he was going half the time, but somehow he never could bring himself to visit. It was almost easier to bear the cruelty of boys his own age than the pity of men, the way they'd look at him sometimes with regret, the unaccustomed tenderness that crept into their voices when they asked him how he was getting on.

Until his illness, Peter had never imagined anything for himself but a life on the water, hauling nets, catching fish; to him that was the measure of a man. But now he would never be part of any crew. A little hand lining, a little jigging, no more than the oldest of fishermen could do, that was all that was left of the life he had wanted.

Because of the sickness. It had started slowly and took a long time to settle in Peter's leg. Then there were operations, relapses and complications that dragged on for a year and a half, then, finally, his slow recovery. At first, it took time and effort to even walk again, for Peter had spent so much time in bed that his muscles wouldn't work. But it was enough then to be alive. Just to sit in the sun and feel the wind on his face, to see the high rocky hills and the town spread out before him. To know that he was allowed to remain among the living.

The sickness he remembered as a long, dark tunnel where he had lived one day, then another, then another with no thought beyond survival for that moment. Then, gradually, the kind of time that healthy people take for granted, time that has a future, returned to him. It was only then that he realized that his knee was ruined and his life was changed forever.

Well, there were some blessings to count after all, as his Nan would say. Because they lived in town and his Nan and father worked so hard, he could have an education that might someday provide him with the means to earn a living at work he could like. Someday. But for now, he was like a boat torn loose from its moorings, adrift without direction.

For no reason he could name, his thoughts drifted back to Dr. McCallum's fine, big house where he had been yesterday afternoon, and his classmate Evelyn. She was tall and awkward, always late for everything, her uniform askew, her dark, curly hair falling into her eyes. She might be halfway pretty if she'd laugh or smile. But Peter suddenly realized, in the two months since school started, he had not seen her smile once.

He supposed he ought to envy a girl like that anyway, living in such a house. He didn't. She seemed lost. She had some friends, if someone like Letty Winsor could be called a friend, but she was still the only other person in the class who was as out of place as Peter. He might have taken some comfort in that, looking down on her. He couldn't. In spite of the big house full of people, she seemed alone. It wasn't likely he could ever get close to her, the differences between them being what they were, but he would have been happy to look out for her, to be her friend.

He sighed. These days, I seem to spend my whole life longing after things I can't possibly have, he thought. What's wrong with me?

November was mild this year but the dampness bothered him after a bit, and he made his way back to the house. He was pleased to find it empty except for his grandmother. Now that he was growing older, he didn't like to admit to the surge of tenderness he felt at the sight of her. She was the only mother he had ever known and now she seemed so old and frail. The balance between them was shifting; where once she had taken care of Peter, he was more often the one to care for her these days. She looked up and smiled as he came in, then put her knitting aside, reached over and turned off the radio.

"Is there a cup of tea left?" he asked.

"There's still some fresh milk. I'll make you some cocoa," she replied, "You needs your nourishment Peter."

"Sit where you are, Nan, I'll look after it myself," and he made some for both of them.

She watched as he fetched the cups and poured the milk. "Peter, you're after growing some fast. I mind the times I used to take you berry picking with me, up over the hill," she said. "How frightened you'd be of the fairies. You used to think they'd taken your mother away, you see." She paused and Peter realized she still could not recover from the sadness that the only woman she'd ever lost in childbirth should be her own daughter. Then she smiled. "I used to fill your pockets with bread, turn your socks inside out, everything I could think of to ease your mind. Finally, your father got a five cent piece, put a hole through the centre and we strung that around your neck, so the silver would keep the fairies off. Even then, you'd never stray from me."

He tried to smile with her but, to his surprise, the memory still frightened him. It was as if a cold hand had touched the back of his neck. "Well, sure, we know there's no such thing as fairies now, don't we Nan?" he asked, wanting her to reassure him.

"Peter, my son," she said, "There's more things in heaven and earth than you or I could know. When I was just a girl, no older than you are now, I'd go up alone on Signal Hill and sometimes I'd hear music. Sad, beautiful music from a tin whistle that could make you want to laugh and cry all at once. There was some said that the music must come from a ship in the harbour and it was just a trick of echoes off the rocks. But others told stories of those who followed that music and went astray. Some was never seen again. Others never were right in the head afterwards. Now they said those ones was switched out there, that it wasn't themselves who came back at all, but some fairy person. Others said it was the shock of what they saw that drove them mad."

Peter put a mug in front of his grandmother and sat down, forcing himself to smile. "Don't go getting all foolish in your old age Nan. You never used to talk like this."

"When you was little Peter, you always scared too easy for such talk. Not that you're a coward," she added, "No one who watched you fight your illness could ever say that of you, my son. 'Twas only anything unnatural, fairies, ghosts and the like that frightened you. I remembers when old

Ches Barrett told you how his brother came back to tell him where his savings was hid after he'd lost his life on the *Florizel*." She chuckled. "You slept in my bed for a month after that."

Peter blushed deeply at the thought. "Sure, I wasn't even six at the time."

"Perhaps not," his Nan conceded. "Which reminds me. I saw Ches Barrett today. He was wondering if you'd be by to help him work on that new skiff he's making for his son-in-law. To hear him tell it, there's not a soul in St. John's he'd trust to help mould out the timbers of a vessel but you."

Peter flushed with pleasure. Uncle Ches Barrett was the only man who never pitied him his handicap, always expecting Peter to do his fair share of the work. He knew more about boat building than anyone Peter knew, and, as his Nan said, seemed happy of Peter's help.

"Perhaps I'll have some time tomorrow. Will you be needing me?"

"I means to go to the public health clinic on Duckworth Street. I'm out of birth certificates. Then I wants to do some shopping. I thought you might come along to help carry my parcels. You could visit the library while I'm at the clinic. I'll only take an hour or so." The library and public health clinic were both housed in a big brick building that had once been a museum.

"If we go in the morning, there'll be time enough for me to help Uncle Ches as well."

"Good, that's settled then. Now, I'll be off to bed. Turn out the lamp when you comes up, Peter and don't forget to take your tonic," she said and she made her way up the narrow stairs.

When she was gone, Peter turned off the lamp, then lifted the dark green blackout blinds on the windows. He looked out over the harbour, back towards St. John's. There was hardly a light to be seen and the city looked eerie in the darkness. Then, ignoring the bottle of tonic by the sink, he followed his Nan upstairs.

In bed a few minutes later, he was just drifting into sleep, dreaming of the sun on the water, when a faint sound jerked him back into consciousness. He listened, suddenly alert. Wasn't that music? Sweet, haunting music? But there was nothing, only the rising wind. Don't be so foolish, he told himself, rolled over and went to sleep.

Chapter Four

When Ev woke up the next morning, she wondered what to do. She didn't want to go with her grandmother to the Women's Patriotic Association. Letty and Doris were sure to be there, and besides, the other women gossiped endlessly about this one missing in action and that one lost at sea until Ev had nightmares. "I won't go any more," Ev said out loud. "I just can't."

Then she remembered the vanity table. More than a day had passed without her grandmother noticing, but it was just a matter of time until she did. Well, there was no use worrying about that yet. At least on Saturday the horrible blue tunics stayed in the closet. When Ev got up, she chose a white and green plaid skirt and a white wool pullover. The skirt was full with small, shallow pockets. Ev didn't usually care what she wore, but this skirt made her feel light and airy. She took the knife from under her pillow and put it into one of the pockets. It just fit.

Her grandmother was waiting at the dining room table. Ev knew as soon as she saw her grandmother that the leg of the vanity had not been noticed yet. "Hurry along Evelyn," she said, "I want to get there as soon as possible. We've received a new shipment of wool, finally."

"Grandmother, I don't want to go."

"Oh." Her grandmother was clearly taken aback. "I thought you enjoyed your Saturdays with Letty and Doris."

"Well, I just. . . I just feel like being alone today." Ev didn't like to think of herself as a liar. It was hard to meet her grandmother's eyes.

"If that's the way you feel, you're certainly too old to be dragged," her grandmother said, "I would have thought you'd do everything you could to help the war effort." Those words stung Ev. She sat staring at her plate until her grandmother finally turned away and left the dining room. Ev realized her grandmother had probably enjoyed showing her off, the brave daughter of her brave son who was overseas. So I probably didn't need to use the knife on the vanity at all, she thought.

While Ev ate breakfast, she thought about how much she hated the weekends. She had long since given up the idea of exploring the city; her grandmother said it was too dangerous for a young girl to be out alone on the weekends with all these servicemen about, and no one had argued with her. Ev thought about sneaking out alone, but her grandparents knew too many people. She was certain to be caught. Ev's mother, of course, was resting. This was bound to be a boring day. Perhaps she could slip down to the basement after Millie finished the breakfast dishes and look for some glue. It might be possible to repair the leg of the vanity before anyone noticed. Maybe later when Millie was upstairs vacuuming.

Ev had just settled down in the parlour with her father's book when her grandfather passed the door, saw her and stopped. "Evelyn, you don't plan to spend the whole day cooped up in here do you?"

Ev nodded, knowing her grandfather had probably forgotten that she wasn't allowed out alone.

"Well, that will never do. I have my hours at the public health clinic on Duckworth Street under the library. You're fond of books. Get your library card and come with me."

"Grandpa, I don't have a library card," she said.

He looked at her with surprise, then spoke as if he was talking to someone who wasn't there. "We've been so preoccupied worrying about Duncan and Nina," he said. Then, the usual briskness came back into his voice. "You'll have one today, my lass. Get your coat and come. I haven't got all day." And he was gone to the car, coattails flying, expecting Ev to follow in his wake. She didn't need to be asked twice.

When Ev entered the garage, her grandfather

sat waiting in the car he called his only indulgence. Her grandfather's big green Packard was the nicest car Ev had ever seen. She always felt snug and protected inside its huge, plush body. If he wasn't a doctor he probably wouldn't even be able to drive it around now, since gas was rationed and this car used so much. Usually, Ev rode in the Packard only when they went to church on Sundays, sitting in the back seat. Now she was allowed to sit right up in front where her grandmother always sat.

Downtown was a steady downhill descent from Ev's grandparents' house, and the Packard took the steep hills like some sleek, surefooted beast. Ev's grandfather talked to her as he drove. "You know Ev, I didn't need Mrs. Bursey's opinion about your mother, exactly, although it was perfectly sound. She's such a gentle old soul, I thought her company might do your mother some good."

"And it did too," Ev said, "She was right cheerful until Grandmother started in about the pie." Immediately, Ev knew she'd said the wrong thing, but to her surprise, her grandfather didn't chide her.

"Yes, well, your grandmother is less than sympathetic, I know. She never has taken to the company of other women. I was glad when Duncan was born a boy." An embarrassed silence followed leaving Ev to wonder how her grandparents had felt when she was born.

Although she hardly ever saw him alone, her grandfather was turning out to be someone Ev could talk to. She wondered if she could tell him about the vanity table. But no, how could she? If she told him, he would know what a horrible person she really was, and then he wouldn't like her at all. At least she could ask him about the war. Most of the time, Ev couldn't look at the newspapers or listen to the radio broadcasts that everyone else was glued to. She knew she was being silly, like a little kid hiding her eyes from something that scared her, but it wasn't anything she could change. Of course, everyone talked about the war all the time, so even if Ev didn't want to know, she heard things. The African theatre, the fighting in Italy, it all frightened her more because she only half understood what people were talking about. Her grandparents didn't know this. They thought she was too young to understand what was going on. But now she wanted to know.

"Grandpa," she said, "Are we going to win the war?"

Ian McCallum hesitated. "Well, honestly Evelyn, if you'd asked me that a few weeks back, I couldn't have said it looked very good. That was a terrible defeat at Dieppe this summer. But things seem to be turning around, with the new offensive in North Africa and all. Now, we have real reason to hope that our side will gain the upper hand, not that this will happen tomorrow, you understand," he said.

Why couldn't he just lie and tell me we'll win the war, Ev thought. But at least it was a grown-up answer. The kind her father would have given.

It was a lovely, mild day, more like September than November. Released from the company of the boring ladies of the WPA and Letty and Doris, Ev felt like someone let out of prison. Across the calm waters of the harbour, the Southside Hills towered in the weak morning sun. The old museum building stood at the bottom of a steep street, and just for a moment Ev could imagine them driving right inside, smashing the glass and upsetting everything.

They didn't, of course. Her grandfather parked the car then fetched his doctor's black bag from the back seat. "The library is upstairs Ev. The children's section is on the left," he said. "I'm amazed no one thought to bring you here before. Get a library card. Then you'll be able to take out some books."

Her grandfather went into the public health clinic on the first floor and Ev went up the stairs. At the top of the first flight, an Eskimo kayak was suspended in midair over an open space, the only indication that this building had once been a museum.

Inside the library, Ev was met by shelf after high shelf of books. She stopped and caught her breath. She had grown up in small communities, a few years here and there, wherever her father was needed to supervise hydroelectric construction projects. She had never lived in a place with a library, so she hadn't even considered coming to this one. There were always plenty of books at home, of course, ordered specially from Water Street bookstores for Christmas or birthdays or sometimes just when her father thought she should have some. But the idea of being able to choose any book from these many shelves was almost dizzying. She breathed the musty smell of old books deeply, wondering where to begin.

"May I help you?" The voice cut into her reverie. A woman she had not noticed was sitting at a desk, examining her. Her hair was tightly waved, and she seemed cautious, as if someone might be about to run off with a book.

"Yes please, I'd like a library card," Ev said. She didn't like the way this lady looked at her.

"Certainly. I'm afraid you'll need to have your mother or father sign it before you can take out books."

"'Could my grandfather? He's just downstairs in the public health clinic."

"Oh!" the librarian said.

From the comfortable chair where he sat, Peter recognized the disapproval in that sound. Dressed in her old fall coat, Ev could easily have come from a poor family. Peter knew Mrs. Noseworthy, the librarian, imagined that Ev's grandfather was a patient at the public health clinic. He also guessed that Ev had no idea how that would make her look to Mrs. Noseworthy who was not a mean woman, but snobbish. The situation annoyed him so much that he rose and came over.

"Hello, Evelyn," he said, surprised at his own boldness. "I never knew Doctor McCallum had public health clinic on Saturdays."

It was Mrs. Noseworthy who replied. "Why

yes, Peter, he certainly does. The poor of this city are lucky indeed to receive the care of a doctor of his calibre." Then she turned to Ev. "You mean to say that Doctor McCallum is your grandfather?"

Ev nodded.

"Oh," she said again, but this time her voice was filled with approval. "He certainly may sign for your card, my dear. You should have told me. Why, you must be Duncan's daughter. I remember your father. You're just the spit of him, now that I look at you. And what's your name?"

As Peter watched, Ev smiled at the librarian. The mention of her father's name seemed to transform her. "Evelyn, Miss," she said.

"Just call me Mrs. Noseworthy, my dear," the librarian replied, and she began to type up a library card for Ev.

Peter stood uncomfortably by. Ev seemed to be ignoring him. He realized it was probably more awkwardness than rudeness on her part, but that didn't help much. He was just about to return to his chair when Mrs. Noseworthy pulled the card from the typewriter and spoke to him.

"Peter, you know these shelves as well as I do and I've got new books to shelf-list. Show Evelyn around for me please?"

Ev followed Peter around the shelves without saying anything. Ordinarily, silence didn't bother Peter, but there was something about Ev's silence that made him jittery, so finally he spoke. "What kind of books do you like?" he asked.

"Oh, adventure stories best. A few weeks ago I finished *Kidnapped*. Have you ever read it?"

Peter smiled and jerked his head towards the chair he'd left when Ev came in. "Just started it this morning. Come here while I shows you where Stevenson's books are to," he said, and he did.

When Ev had chosen her books, she settled into a chair not too far from Peter's. They read silently, as they were required to do in the library, both relieved to know they didn't have to think of words to say to each other. But, although neither would have admitted it, they were happier than they would have been alone.

They were so absorbed in their books that they did not see Mrs. Bursey until she was standing next to Peter. "Well, youngsters," she said softly, "Found each other did you? Dr. McCallum imagined you would when I told him Peter was up here." Then she turned to Ev. "Your grandfather thought you might enjoy coming round to the shops with us rather than spending the whole morning up here alone, Evelyn. He said we could stop back at noon. He has some patients to see at the Battery, and he's offered to drive Peter and myself home then."

After Ev had taken her library card down to be signed and placed her books in her grandfather's car, she and Peter and Mrs. Bursey went down the courthouse steps that led from Duckworth Street to Water Street. There, Ev noticed that some of the shops had big boards where the plate glass windows should have been. Was this some sort of blackout protection? Ev had to know.

"What happened to those windows?" she said.

"Servicemen," Peter replied in his usual

abrupt way. "They break up the windows. Shop-keepers give up replacing them after a while. Easier to board 'em over, they thinks."

"Yes, my child," Mrs. Bursey added. "Some wild lot these servicemen are. The city never was like this before, not in my time in any case. A young girl like yourself is hardly safe out alone these days."

"I know," Ev said, and she could not keep the bitterness from her voice. "Grandmother won't allow me out alone except to walk to school. This is the first time I've been downtown since we came here in September."

"My, how do you pass the weekends my child?" Mrs. Bursey asked in surprise.

"I was going to the WPA with Doris Piercy and Letty Winsor on Saturdays," Ev said, "But I really don't like them, especially Letty." Ev was surprised by how easy it was to say this.

Behind his grandmother, Peter smiled.

"I suppose now I'll just stay home and read," Ev continued. "Since I'm not allowed out alone."

"Goodness, child, you'll ruin your health, shut up like that all the time. Let me talk to your grandfather to see if he won't let you spend the afternoon with us out to the Battery. The fresh air will do you some good and Peter can show you around."

"But Nan," Peter protested, "I'm helping Ches Barrett with that skiff he's starting on, remember?" Ches Barrett wouldn't be pleased if Peter showed up with Ev in tow, and Peter wasn't willing to give up an afternoon's work on the skiff.

"Peter, I'm surprised at you," Mrs. Bursey said. She said nothing more. She didn't have to. Her disapproval was so rare and weighed so heavily on Peter that it never failed to bring him around to her way of seeing things.

"I'm sorry Nan," he said after a minute. "You're certainly welcome to come with me this afternoon, Evelyn, if you wants to watch some boat building."

Ev wanted nothing more than to spend the afternoon outdoors, away from the stifling boredom of her grandparents' house. But Peter seemed to be inviting her only to please his grandmother. She was so hurt and annoyed that she ignored Peter, turning to his grandmother instead. "Yes, Mrs. Bursey, I'd like it very much if you would speak to Grandpa for me." And she walked up the street without looking at Peter.

In the shops, Peter and Ev followed Mrs. Bursey. "I wants to make some mittens for Effie's three," Mrs. Bursey said, "What do you think, Peter?"

"Might as well," he replied, "You haven't made them any since last fall. Remember? That was the first time you tried that snowflake pattern."

"So it was," Mrs. Bursey said.

Ev felt a catch in her throat, listening to Peter and his Nan talk. That's what holds people together, she thought, knowing what someone did yesterday or last year, knowing what they plan to do tomorrow. This was something that Ev had taken for granted until a few months ago. She didn't share that kind of closeness with anyone now.

Mrs. Bursey turned to her. "Wool is some hard to come by these days, what with everyone knitting for the soldiers overseas," she said. "I mean to make Peter a pair of mittens too, before the weather turns cold. What do you think of these colours Evelyn?" she asked. She held bright red and blue wool.

"Oh, those are little kids' colours, Mrs. Bursey," Ev said. "I think the navy is better for someone as old as Peter, or the brown."

When Mrs. Bursey had gone to pay for the wool Ev looked up to see Peter smiling at her. "She'd have me decked out in mitts with clowns on them likely as not if you didn't stop her." Then he laughed. When he did, he looked like a mischievous little boy. Ev laughed with him.

When they returned to the bottom of the courthouse steps, Ev wondered how Mrs. Bursey and Peter would ever climb those many steep flights. Still, she knew Peter would never admit the effort it would cost him to make that climb. Ev turned to Peter and said, "Why don't you stay here with your Nan and help her mind her parcels while I get Grandpa? He and I can drive down here and pick you both up. That will be easier."

All Peter said was, "That's a good idea." But she could see from his eyes how grateful he was. Ev went flying up the courthouse steps and into the public health clinic where she ran to her grandfather laughing and breathless. "I left Peter and his Nan at the bottom of the steps," she explained.

"My goodness, Evelyn, I hardly knew you,"

her grandfather said, "Well, lass, you seem to be enjoying yourself."

"Oh yes, Grampa," Ev said as they walked out to the car. "And Mrs. Bursey said I could spend the afternoon with her and Peter. Could I? Please."

"I don't see why not. I'm sure I trust them to take good care of you. Just so long as you call me for a ride home well before blackout time."

Ev climbed into her grandfather's Packard and they drove towards Water Street. There, Mrs. Bursey settled into the front seat of the car, and Ev climbed into the back with Peter. As they drove towards the Battery, Ev rolled down her window a little. The breeze carried the scent of the ocean in to her. It was like coming home.

"Who are you going to visit this afternoon Doctor McCallum?" Mrs. Bursey asked.

"Nancy Mercer's baby has the chicken pox," Ev's grandfather replied. "And she's as nervous as a first-time mother will be about such things, so I thought I'd call in on her."

"Oh, I know, I've been over there myself twice this week," Mrs. Bursey said.

"And old Chesley Barrett's rheumatism is bothering him," Ev's grandfather continued. "He finds it difficult to get around sometimes so I thought I'd kill two birds with one stone."

"Ev will meet Ches this afternoon in any case," Mrs. Bursey said, "Since Peter is helping him build a vessel."

"Is that so Peter?" Dr. McCallum glanced at him in the rear view mirror. "Well, Ev, you'll find Ches Barrett interesting enough if he takes a liking to you. He's the seventh son of a seventh son. You know what that means?"

"Not really Grandpa," Ev said.

"Well, I'd better let Mrs. Bursey tell you. She knows more about these things than I do, I'm sure."

"Well now, there's some says the seventh son has special powers, to heal and such. And certainly Ches can do that for some problems and he gets feelings about things from time to time. There's some fear him for that, but more respect him, for he's never used his power to do harm as another man might."

"Do you believe in such things, Mrs. Bursey?" Dr. McCallum asked.

"Well Doctor, I'm hardly a one for magic." She laughed softly under her breath, "With women in childbirth, I've learned to put my trust in God and doctors when nature goes astray. But I've known Ches all my life and I must say there's things he's done and had happened to him I'd find hard to explain."

At that moment, a chill breeze blew through the window. Ev shivered.

Chapter Five

The road to the outer battery was narrowly wedged between a high rock cliff and a sheer drop to the water. Ev held her breath as her grandfather's big car eased along. Around a bend beyond that dangerous-looking stretch of road, a small cluster of houses lay close together with fishing stores and stages on the rocks facing the sea. Noisy gulls wheeled over the white boats moored in the water below.

Mrs. Bursey insisted Peter and Ev eat dinner while Ev's grandfather made his calls. The Tilley house was small and crowded but comfortable. It felt more like home to Ev than her grandparents' big house. In the kitchen, two big windows faced the harbour and the whole city spread out before Ev's eyes.

"Oh my," Ev said. "It's beautiful here. It must be fun to sit and watch the ships going by." She turned to Peter and smiled at him, her shyness gone. She didn't seem much like the silent, awkward girl in the library that morning.

"Yes, child," Mrs. Bursey said as she put the kettle on. "We always loved to see the harbour lights at night, didn't we Peter? Now, with this blackout on there's no lights to see. Everything's after changing." She sighed, then began to make dinner.

Dr. McCallum's Packard was parked in the narrow road outside Ches Barrett's house when Ev and Peter arrived there half an hour later. Peter didn't knock at the door, he just opened it and walked in. Ev hadn't seen anyone do that since she'd left Belbin's Cove. It made her feel at home and homesick all at once, and somehow closer to Peter. He isn't really from town at all, Ev thought. The Battery is like a little outport perched on the rocks beside St. John's.

This house was larger than the one Peter lived in, but dark and not half as clean. A sour smell hung in the air. Something else hung there too, an uneasy feeling that someone might be lurking in the shadows. In the kitchen, dirty dishes were piled high in the sink and houseflies buzzed around. One landed on an open jam jar on the table. Ev's grandfather sat nearby with an old man whom Ev guessed was Mr. Barrett.

He was small and round with wispy white hair and a pink face. When he turned to look at the newcomers, Ev noticed his eyes. They were clear, pale blue, blue as the shadowy part of an iceberg. They were eyes that could see far into the distance, into the future, or into a person's heart.

When Ches saw Peter and Ev, he smiled, his eyes disappearing into a sea of wrinkles. "Took your time getting here, Peter my son," he said, but there was a smile in his voice as well. "And this must be young Evelyn. Your grandfather here tells me you came in from Belbin's Cove. I remembers Belbin's Cove from the days I sailed with Captain Reg Piercey out of Winterton. You knows Winterton I'm sure." Ev nodded. He was the first person she had met in St. John's who knew anything about the place she thought of as home. She waited to hear more.

"Yes my dear," Ches Barrett continued, a faraway look coming into those farseeing eyes. "I was a lad in those days, hardly older than you are now Peter. There was a maid in Belbin's Cove, Sally Trimm, I used to walk with now and again. Saucy as a gull, she was. You knows where The Point is too, of course," he said to Ev. She nodded again, and suddenly she could picture the grassy point of land beyond Belbin's Cove where white rocks sloped gently down to the sea. It was one of the places she'd loved best. But this was more than a thought. It was almost as if this old man's memory had carried her home.

"Sally'd take me there in summer to pick them black mossberries. You mind how the mossberries grows all around there? The scent of them right heavy in the air?" Ev nodded again. Ches Barrett's voice continued, but she lost the meaning of his words. Instead, she felt the sun on her face, the breeze off the sea in her hair. She heard the ragged cry of a tern and saw The Point before her, green with mossberry bushes and low grass, the blue sea bright beyond. At the same time, the dull ache of homesickness in her heart eased. Then suddenly, his voice stopped and she was back in the stale, dark air of the Barrett house. But the feeling of peace stayed with her.

She looked at him and it seemed he knew what his words had done to her. "You'll be back there one day, my maid," he said. "Never fear."

What happened, she wondered. Had he hypnotised her? She should probably be afraid of a man who could do such things, but somehow she knew Mr. Barrett could be trusted.

All this happened so quickly that neither Peter nor Dr. McCallum noticed anything unusual. Ev's grandfather stood up and gathered his black bag briskly. "I'll be off," he said. "I understand you have a boat to build. Now Ev, remember to call me before blackout time." And he was gone.

After he left, Ches Barrett rose stiffly, walking away from the dishes on the table without a backward glance. "Come along, youngsters," he said, "We got to get a start on that skiff." He seemed to take it for granted Ev would spend the afternoon with them.

Ches Barrett's fishing store was much like Peter's father's: a brown wooden shed, mostly empty of nets now. But on one wall hung the many tools of a boat builder, neatly arranged and carefully tended, and a quantity of lumber was stacked on the floor. Ches went to an old bench and cleared the sawdust from it. Ev understood that she was expected to sit there. Then he turned to Peter. "Bring me the moulds lad," he said.

From the wall Peter took a device that looked like three curved rulers, loosely joined together. "Now fetch me some plank stock." Ev watched as Peter brought the lumber. Ches adjusted the thing he called the moulds and laid it on one of the boards, then Peter traced a curved pattern onto the wood with a pencil. "Mind you keep the moulds just where I lays them to, my son," Ches said to Peter. "We got to keep that curve suent." Ev didn't know what that meant. Together, Peter and the old man repeated their actions again and again, marking out the timbers of the vessel.

Ev sat forgotten. This wasn't what she wanted at all. After a few minutes she said, "Can't I do something to help?"

"You'll watch," Ches said shortly. "That's help enough for now."

"But I want to do something," Ev insisted.

"Peter, lad, how long did you have to watch before I let you help me?"

Peter grinned. "Six years, I'd say. Maybe seven."

Ev was furious. No one treated her like this. She gave a little flounce of anger on the bench and when she did, the knife fell from her shallow skirt pocket onto the bare plank floor. Ches, who was standing near her, bent down and picked it up.

"This is a fine knife," he said. "Yours, is it?"

Ev nodded shortly. "My father gave it to me."

The knife was her secret. She wanted to snatch it back from him, but he held on to it, turning it in his hand.

"A knife is a queer thing, isn't it? It can be useful, or it can do harm. Whatever its owner wants."

Ev was sure that Ches knew about the knife. She kept her head down and nodded. Give it back and leave me alone, she thought. It belongs to me.

"Ever make anything with this knife?" Ches asked.

Ev raised her eyes and looked at him. He wasn't teasing now.

"My father was going to teach me, before he went away," she said, "But he didn't have time."

"Peter, I think you knows what you're about there," Ches said. Then he turned to Ev. "Let me show you a thing or two with this knife of yours." He took a small stick of wood from the table beside him and opened the knife blade. He tapered the stick at one end, then carefully made a diamond-shaped notch near the other end on one side of the stick. "Think you can do that?" he asked. Ev nodded. He took his pencil from behind his ear and made seven marks up the side of the stick. "Let me see you make seven more of them, then, just as I did. And mind you don't break the stick." Then he returned to Peter.

It looked easy but the knife wouldn't do what Ev wanted. First it cut too deeply and then it wouldn't cut at all. She pushed hard and the stick snapped in two. When that happened, Ev thought she was going to cry, but when she looked up, Peter was watching. "That's what happened to me the first time too," he said.

"That's so," said Ches, marking another stick with his pencil for Ev, "But you were only eight as I recall."

I'll do better this time, Ev thought, and she did. She was on the sixth notch before the stick broke. "Oh, damn," she cried.

"None of that language in here," Ches said, but he had to turn his head away so Ev wouldn't see him smile.

This time, Peter came over and marked the stick. "Third time lucky," he said. And he was right. Ev made all eight notches. They weren't the same size or depth, but they were all there and the stick was still in one piece.

"Now what?" Ev asked.

"Now you watch," Ches said. "If you wants to know something about boat building, you watch."

This time, Ev watched without protesting. She snapped the blade of the knife shut, but didn't feel she had to hide it in her pocket any more.

It was pleasant to be here, in the warm afternoon, with the smell of the sea and fresh lumber, watching Peter and Ches work together. They made an odd pair. Peter was already taller than Ches. He took instruction from the old man and marked the wood, his straight brown hair falling down into his eyes, his concentration intense and his movements sure. Just for a moment, Ev caught a glimpse of the graceful, strong man he

would have become but for his illness. She felt a
pang of loss, but quickly pushed it aside. Peter
might want her friendship, but not her pity.

After an hour more Ches stopped, asking Peter
to stack the marked lumber. Peter protested.
"Sure we only just started Uncle Ches. The skiff'll
never get built at this speed."

Ches chuckled. "Peter, you always got a head
of steam up, don't you now? We got all winter
ahead to build this boat, and I'm not a youngster
like yourself. Besides, 'tis not much fun for
Evelyn to be sitting here just watching us. You
should show her around before it gets too late."
Then he turned to Ev. "Show me your work," he
said. Ev was surprised to see that her hand shook
as she gave him the stick. She wanted him to like
what she had done, to say that she'd done well.

"Well, I've seen better," Ches said, "But I've
seen worse as well. Give me your knife, maid."

Ev handed him the knife, this time without
regret. It wasn't a shameful secret any more, just
a knife her father had given to her, and she'd used
it to make. . . something, whatever it was. Ches
tapered the end that was not notched, then began
to whittle away at a smaller piece of wood.
Turning to Peter, he said, "Peter, go ask your
Nan for a straight pin." Peter obeyed without
comment.

When he left, Ches looked at Ev. She felt as if
those pale blue eyes were looking right into her.
She wanted to hide. "I'll teach you how to use
this knife, if you comes along with Peter, and
you'll use it like I shows you, won't you, my

maid?" Ches said. There was something gentle in his voice that made Ev want to cry again, not with anger or frustration this time, but with relief.

"Yes," Ev said, "If you want me to I will."

"That's good," Ches said. When Peter returned with the pin, Ches bored a hole, barely bigger than the pin, into the small piece of wood he had whittled. Then, taking the stick Ev had notched, he carefully hammered the pin through so that the smaller piece stuck out at right angles. Now it looked like a notched stick with a propeller. "There," he said, holding it up. "What do you think , Peter, my son?"

"Best kind," said Peter.

Ev knew they were teasing her again. Normally she hated being teased, but this was not unkind. "All right, you win," she said, laughing. "What is it?"

"What is it?" Ches said, pretended to be surprised. "Why I don't believe it has a name. Peter, you ever hear anyone call this by a name?"

"No," Peter said, "Can't say that I have."

"Then what does it do?"

In answer, Ches handed Ev his pencil and this thing she had notched. "Rub the pencil along the notches, on one side, mind you."

Ev did. At first, nothing happened, then slowly, the propeller began to turn. She laughed. "Now," Ches said, "Rub the pencil on the other side of the notches." When she did, the propeller changed direction and went the other way.

"The vibrations make it turn," Peter explained.

"There," Ches said, "Now you knows how to do something useful with that knife of yours." His stress on the word useful made Ev laugh again.

"This isn't exactly useful," she said.

"Not in itself perhaps, but you learned how to notch the wood without breaking it. That's how I started Peter, and how my own father started me as well. You practice with that knife, get some straight pins, see if you can make me one of those from scratch yourself before next weekend. I can't promise I'll ever make a boat builder out of you. Not yet at any rate. But you keep at it and we'll see how far you get. Now, I wants my pipe. Show Ev around, Peter. My rodney's still in the water. Come back for it after a while my son."

Outside, the afternoon sun shone brightly. Ahead, where the road ended, Ev could see a path heading out towards the open sea.

"Where does that path go?" Ev asked.

"Out along the rocks past the Narrows," Peter said. "There's a cave out there, runs right down the rock face and into the sea. But we can't go there no more. They built a gun battery just beyond the houses and the path's off limits now. We can go up here a ways though," he added, indicating a narrow footpath winding up through the houses. "There's a place to sit at the top."

She followed Peter up the steep path. He walked slowly, dragging his right leg a little. Ev could see the climb was difficult for him, even with his cane. He took her out beyond the houses and they sat on some rocks looking out at the city. Below her, ships of all sizes floated near the long wooden finger piers that reached into the silver water of the harbour. Beyond that, wooden houses spilled over the hills like coloured children's blocks. The sun was warm on her face. On such a day, it almost seemed possible to Ev that she might learn to like St. John's.

She spoke quickly now, to keep an awkward silence from coming between them. "What was that thing Mr. Barrett called the moulds?" she asked.

Peter smiled. "You might call him Uncle Ches. Everyone does, although he's not a relative of ours. The moulds is, well, it's something used in boat building. I suppose you knows as much by now," he said, smiling again. "Those three parts can be adjusted to give you the shape of most parts of a vessel. That's important. Say you don't get the right curve, the right amount of hollowing we calls it, in the timbers we moulded out today. The vessel won't be safe to use, she won't sit firm in the water. The curve has to be what we calls suent, that is to say a proper curve." Peter's usual reticence was gone. It was surprising to hear him talk so long and so fluently. "The moulds we used today was made by Uncle Ches's great grandfather and passed along to him. It's promised to me now, seeing as how there's no one in the Barrett family taking up the skill."

"And what will you do next?" Ev asked.

"Those timbers will have to be shaped out and there's other parts still we needs to collect. Uncle Ches likes green wood whenever we can get it.

Some things, like the plank stock we used today, have to be bought, but other parts we finds in the woods."

"I thought you'd want wood that was dry," she said, surprised.

"Not at all. The dry wood gets the water into it, you see? The green wood, spruce and fir we use, is still full of gum. That keeps the water out. That's better." Suddenly Peter laughed. "But I never knew a girl to be so interested in boat building," he said. It annoyed Ev to see him teasing her again. Perhaps he thought she was only asking these questions because she was interested in him.

"Well, my father is an engineer," she said shortly. "I'm used to thinking about how things are put together."

"And where is your father to now? Do you know?" Peter asked.

Ev looked unhappy. "We know he landed in North Africa some time in October. We had one letter, then nothing. Nothing for weeks and weeks." The African Theatre. This was where the heaviest fighting had been for the last few weeks. It was in the newspapers and on the radio almost every day. "When I think about it," Ev added, almost in a whisper, "I get really scared."

They sat silent for a moment. Then Peter said, "I don't understand why he went."

If anyone else had said that, even Peter himself a few hours before, Ev would have lost her temper. Now she answered quietly. "No one else does either. Only me." She hesitated. Could the understanding she had of her father be put into words?

"You see, he says you can't leave the important things to everyone else and expect them to get done. When he realized how dangerous this war is, how much will be lost if we lose, he said he couldn't not go. Can you understand that?"

"I'm not sure. How could he leave you and your mother the way he did?" Peter hesitated. "Especially with your mother. . ." his voice trailed off.

Ev stood up and turned away. She was embarrassed and angry, partly because Peter was asking her things she asked herself over and over. "He's doing this for us. Don't you see? My mother didn't know about the baby until after my father enlisted. It was too late then for him to change things. And anyway, my mother wasn't like this before. She's useless now, she's just given up." When she turned back to Peter, her voice shook with anger. "You think he doesn't care for us, that he ran away. It wasn't like that at all."

"I'm sorry, Evelyn," Peter said, "I never meant to hurt your feelings."

If he had tried to defend himself or argue with her, she would have walked down the hill and home. But his straightforwardness disarmed her. The anger faded and she sat down again. "It's all right. You only said what everyone else is thinking. I shouldn't have lost my temper."

"Let's go back down and get Uncle Ches's boat," Peter offered, "We can jig for tires in the harbour."

Ev looked at him in surprise. "Jig for tires?"

The disbelief on her face made Peter laugh.

"There's always some tires at the bottom of the harbour, lost from wharves or thrown in. We can jig them up and give them in for scrap rubber, to help the war effort."

"I never heard of such a thing."

Peter rose. "It's fun, and we should be out on the water on such a fine day. Come on."

They went down the steep path to the Barrett wharf, and Ches was there, sitting out in the sun on a wooden kitchen chair, smoking his pipe. His boat was moored away from the wharf on an anchored line; even in the harbour the seas were too unpredictable to leave a large boat tied to a wharf.

"The old flat is down by the slipway," he said, indicating a smaller row boat.

Peter let Ev get into the flat first, then pushed it away from the slipway. It only took a moment to row out to the larger rodney. Peter moored the flat to the same line. He knew exactly what he was doing and seemed as at home on the water as he was on land.

"You get in first," he said. "I'll hold the flat to." He expertly brought the two boats together, and, holding the gunwale of the larger boat, offered Ev his other hand. "Step lively now," Peter said. Ev climbed into the larger boat. "Now you'll have to hold the flat for me," he said, and with her help he climbed aboard as well. "Once I could jump that with no help at all," he said when they were settled in.

Peter didn't row this bigger boat, but took his place at the stern where he began to work a sculling oar. "Easier than rowing in such a small space as this," he said, and he began to work the single small oar back and forth. The boat responded to his touch with an agility Ev would not have thought possible. "Now, look over into the water and tell me when you spots a tire."

Ev did. At first, she could only see her own face staring back at her. Then she began to make out shapes on the bottom. There was lots of garbage. After a minute she saw something round. "There's one."

Peter came forward with a stout metal hook on a rope. "You try first," he offered. It was hard work to get the tires hooked. Sometimes they'd fall off half way up. He was much better at it, of course, but he was patient with Ev and never mocked her lack of skill.

Ev finally hooked one. "Easy," Peter coached her, "Steady on now." And they had it. Cold and slimy, it slipped out of their hands and drifted back down to the bottom just as they began to lift it out of the water. They laughed so hard they couldn't move. In the end, they only managed to bring up two tires.

Finally, Peter looked up at the sky. "Blackout time soon," he said. "We better get you in."

Chapter Six

When Ev returned to her grandparents' house that evening, it was hard to believe only hours had passed since she'd left. So much had happened. Finally, she thought, I have a real friend. She rushed into the kitchen to tell Millie, who was reading the Saturday paper while supper cooked on the stove.

"Just look at these new party dresses they got down to Ayre's," Millie greeted her, holding up the paper. "They're some pretty, aren't they? Five dollars and eighty cents. Perhaps I'll save that much before all the Christmas dances starts." She sighed as she looked at the ad.

Ev knew almost every cent Millie earned went to her mother, a widow in Harbour Grace with younger children. Ev couldn't imagine what it must be like to have to work so hard, but Millie never seemed sorry for herself.

Ev had no interest in new dresses at Ayre's or

anywhere else, but she sat down across the table from Millie for company. Millie was small and pretty with fluffy blonde hair. Already, at seventeen, she was beginning to show signs of plumpness but for now this gave her graceful, soft curves. She seemed clever enough, but as far as Ev could tell she never had a serious thought in her head. It was all dresses and dates and shoes with Cuban heels.

Before they could talk, Ev's grandmother came into the kitchen. "Oh, hello Evelyn," she said. Then she stood behind Ev's chair, facing Millie. "Mildred," she said, "I'm afraid I'll be taking some money out of your pay this month."

Ev watched the colour drain from Millie's face. "Why Mrs. McCallum, whatever for? I done every bit of work you asked me to."

"Did you vacuum clean our bedroom when I was out today?"

"Yes I did, and tidied it just as neat as could be."

"Then I suppose you know something about this?" She placed a small block of varnished wood on the table, split and raw on one side. Ev stayed perfectly still, hoping no one would look at her. It was hard to breathe.

"No, Missus, I never seen that before."

"Well, it was knocked off the leg of my vanity table this afternoon. By the vacuum cleaner, I imagine. That table was a wedding present from my mother. How could you have been so careless?" Her grandmother's voice vibrated into the back of Ev's chair. Each sentence was pitched higher than the last.

"Really, Missus..." Millie began. Ev couldn't keep her head down any longer. Her eyes met Millie's across the table, and suddenly, the older girl stopped. There was a pause which seemed to last forever, then Millie said, "Perhaps you're right, Mrs. McCallum. I'll try to be more careful from now on."

Behind her, Ev heard her grandmother give out a sigh of pent up rage. "You do so, my girl," she said. "I'll have a talk with my husband to see how we will deal with this." Then she turned and left the kitchen.

Ev sat staring into her lap. She heard the click of her grandmother's shoes on the hall floor, then the only sound was the ticking of the kitchen clock. It had never seemed so loud.

"Are you going to tell me?" Millie asked after a long time. She had a right to be angry, but her voice was calm, even kindly.

Ev shook her head. She started to speak, but nothing came out. She tried again. "I can't," she said, "I can't tell you Millie."

Millie sighed, "You puts me in mind of my little brother, Wesley. Just dives into trouble, Wes does, never thinks of what might happen to him until it's too late."

"You knew it was my fault, Millie. Why didn't you tell her?"

"I got five little brothers and sister, Evelyn. My father's dead now, and it's a sin to speak ill of the dead, I knows, but he was a mean man, with a wicked temper. For as long as I can recall, I was always looking out for the young ones, trying to protect them from my father." She looked at Ev now with a cold pride that Ev had never seen before. "When he died, the minister said to my mother that sometimes God works in mysterious ways. We knew what he meant. The TB killed my father and left us all healthy, and I knows how bad it sounds, but that was a blessing if ever there was one. So, it was enough that your Nan was mad at me, without having her mad at the both of us. I'm accustomed to it, you see. At least I knew she'd never lay her hands on me."

Millie went to the stove leaving Ev to think about what she had said. She tried to imagine her own father hitting her in anger. She couldn't. It was something that never had happened, and never would.

"I guess I'm not the only one with troubles," Ev said after a while.

Millie only laughed. "I guess you're not. Now, wherever did you get to today? I was some surprised to see your Nan come home without you."

"I went out to the Battery with Mrs. Bursey and Peter Tilley," Ev said. "I watched some boat building and Peter and I tried to jig tires off the bottom of the harbour to get rubber for the war effort."

Millie looked at her curiously. "Evelyn McCallum, you're a queer stick. The things you thinks of as fun! But at least you've taken up with a fellow. You'll be a lot happier now that you've got a boyfriend."

"No, no," Ev protested, "It's not like that at all, Millie. Peter's just someone to talk to and do things with. I don't want some fellow swooning all over me." Her nose wrinkled in disgust.

"Have it your way for now Evelyn," Millie said. "A few years more and you'll change your tune."

I certainly hope not, Ev thought. But she knew Millie was probably right. Everyone said it had to happen. Girls got a little older and suddenly they all acted like Letty, wanting boys to notice them. They did silly things to get their attention and fussed with clothes. Ev pictured the desire for romance as a kind of fog that would soon sweep into her life and cloud her brain, perhaps forever. While she sat thinking, a knock came to the kitchen door.

"I'll get that," Millie cried, rushing to the door. Millie was not allowed to have young men call for her at the house. This was Ev's grandmother's rule, but sometimes it was ignored. She opened the back door quickly and there stood an American serviceman in his crisp khaki uniform. He was tall and handsome, with lean, high cheekbones and curly blonde hair. There was something about the way he carried himself that Ev didn't like.

"Get yourself in here Gerry," Millie said. "I'm breaking the blackout laws standing here with this door open. In any case, I'm not free until eight-thirty. You knows as much."

This was the way Millie talked to all her fellows. At first Ev had been a bit shocked, thinking Millie would certainly scare them all away. Then she noticed that most seemed to accept this treatment, and some were amused by it. Not this one, though. As Millie moved away from the door, he grabbed her by the wrist and pulled her back towards him. "Don't talk to me like that," he said. He held her wrist just until her eyes began to widen with fright, then let go, laughing.

"What'd you think, Millie? That I was going to hurt you?" he asked. It didn't seem like much of a joke to Ev and Millie's laughter was weak.

"Gerry," she said, pleading a little now, "The missus don't like me to have callers here. I'm lucky young Evelyn isn't the type to tell tales." When Ev was mentioned, he looked at her and smiled. It was not a friendly smile.

"Have it your way, Millie," he said. "I'll be back." And he was gone. Millie closed the door after him and gave Ev a look that asked her not to speak about what she had just seen.

Ev knew that it was Millie's business who she dated, but she couldn't keep silent. "When did you meet him?" she began cautiously.

"Only a few weeks ago," Millie said. It was clear she didn't want to talk, but Ev persisted.

"Is he always like that with you Millie?" she asked.

Millie spoke rapidly, as if a dam inside of her had burst. "No, well that's the problem. He's often not like that at all. He can be right kind, but then he has this mean streak to him, especially when we're alone. Out in public, at a dance say, he's just as polite as anyone could wish. It's as if he's two different people."

"Millie, he sounds like he's more trouble than

he's worth. Why don't you just stop seeing him?"

"I feels right sorry for him Evelyn. He's never had a proper home. He was reared up in orphanages until he was old enough to join the army. In any case, he has his better side. I think perhaps all he needs is someone to love him. I think he could change." When she spoke like that, her voice went all soft. It's that fog, Ev thought, her mind's gone right cloudy with romance.

There was no point in arguing. Millie would simply say Ev was too young to understand. Ev considered talking to her grandfather, but that seemed too much like telling on Millie. Still, as she helped Millie set the table she decided to keep an eye on this Gerry. She owed Millie that much now.

Ev never liked Saturday supper. She hated pea soup, the standard Saturday night fare, and tonight her mother's empty chair at the table reminded Ev that her problems hadn't disappeared while she was away. After grace, Millie brought in the soup. She moved the bowls from tray to table without spilling any, winked at Ev and disappeared.

"Ian," Ev's grandmother said, "Maude Winsor was telling me about the trouble the servicemen are causing her husband. He's losing hundreds of dollars in stolen merchandise, not to mention the money to repair his plate glass windows almost every week. You'd think something could be done."

"Well Gwen," Ev's grandfather said, "There is talk of getting some religious services going on

Sundays at the recreation centres, at the Red Triangle Club and the Caribou Hut, you'll be pleased to know."

"Perhaps it won't help in any case." Ev's grandmother sighed. "I understand it's only the better class of servicemen who frequent the recreation centres. The rest are downtown in those places, what do they call them?"

"Dives and shebeens," Ev said before she could stop herself. She had no idea what a shebeen might be, but from the way the newspapers were always going on about them they sounded exciting.

Her grandfather laughed, but Ev's grandmother looked shocked. "Really, Evelyn. You pick up the strangest things."

"But Grandpa, what is a shebeen?" Ev had to ask now.

"Just a place where liquor is served illegally, my dear," he replied. "Not nearly so wonderful as you might hope."

When dessert was brought in, Ev's grandmother turned to her. "Well, Evelyn, we certainly could have used your help today. Doris asked after you. Your grandfather tells me you went to the library and spent the afternoon with a classmate."

"Yes Grandmother," Ev replied. In spite of herself, her heart began to pound. She knew her grandmother was still annoyed with her for staying home from the WPA, and Peter Tilley was not someone she was likely to approve of. Ev turned to her grandfather for support. "You know, Grandpa, Peter certainly knows a lot about boat building. He reminded me of father when he talked about the way boats are designed."

Her grandfather smiled. "Yes, Peter reminds me of your father too in some ways. When Duncan was a boy he was very keen on making things, on knowing how they worked. Peter is like that." He got a rare, faraway look in his eyes, and Ev realized he was thinking of her father. "Duncan was gentle too, like Peter is, not wild and noisy like so many boys."

"How old is this Peter Tilley?" Ev's grandmother's voice cut into the conversation.

"Well, he lost two years of school, so I suppose he's fourteen," Ev replied.

"Almost a young man." She looked displeased. "Evelyn, you're a young lady now. I don't think a girl of your age should spend time alone with such a boy. People might talk."

"But Grandmother," Ev protested, "We were hardly alone. We spent the whole afternoon out of doors. He is only a friend." Ev was already getting tired of saying this.

Ev's grandfather usually let his wife decide what was best for Ev, but now he spoke. "Gwen," he said, "I've worked with Mrs. Bursey for years. I've known Peter Tilley all his life. He's a fine boy who's had a hard time. I think we should encourage Evelyn's friendship with him."

"Really Ian. You never think about what people will say. I don't want anyone gossiping about my granddaughter running around with some boy from the Battery. Just think how ashamed I'd be."

Ev's grandfather turned to her. "Evelyn, would

you like to be excused now? Perhaps your mother would like a little visit." Ev knew that her grandfather wanted her out of the room. She was glad to leave, but she couldn't help listening outside the dining room door.

Ev's grandfather rarely spoke about religion, but she knew he was a religious man. In his cluttered study behind the parlour was the huge family Bible that had travelled with generations of McCallums from Scotland to Canada and then to Newfoundland. It was always open, and open to a different place every time Ev saw it.

Sometimes when Ev's grandfather wanted to win a point in an argument with his wife, he'd quote from the Bible, and that's what he did now. "'Who can find a virtuous woman, for her price is far above rubies..,'" he said. "Proverbs. Our Ev is a virtuous girl Gwen, a good and innocent girl. We can trust her. That should be enough for you."

Ev's grandmother wasn't pleased. "I don't know what's gotten into Evelyn. Letty Winsor and Doris Piercy were so nice to her. Letty told me today that Evelyn doesn't want to be friends with her." She sighed. "In any case, it matters what people say Ian, even if you think it doesn't. That boy is common. He comes from poor circumstances and he's a cripple. I can just imagine the gossip."

When her grandfather spoke again, Ev noticed the finely controlled anger in his voice. "That girl has been neglected in this house Gwen. I saw that this morning. Nina is too wrapped up in her own troubles to care for her and we've mostly ignored

her. When I saw her outside today I remembered
what a normal, healthy child is supposed to be
like. We can't keep her locked up like a bird in a
cage." He paused. "Now her choice of friends
may be somewhat eccentric, but I cannot let that
ruin her happiness. You know I almost never
insist, but in this case I must. Evelyn will be
allowed to visit the Battery and she will play
with Peter Tilley." Silence followed. Ev had
never heard her grandfather speak like that
before. It bothered her to think he pitied her, but
she was grateful to him. Her grandmother rang
for Millie to clear the table and Ev tiptoed up the
stairs. To her relief, her mother's light was
already turned off.

When Ev came into the schoolyard on
Monday morning she realized she didn't know
what to say to Peter, or if she should say anything
at all. What if people saw them together and
assumed, as Millie and her grandmother had, that
Peter was her boyfriend? She saw Peter standing
across the yard. When their eyes met they both
quickly looked away. Then the bell rang and
everyone moved towards the door. When Ev
went into the playground at recess, Letty and
Doris turned their backs and walked away. Ev
couldn't bring herself to speak to Peter so she
spent recess by herself.

Tuesday was the same, but that afternoon Mrs.
Bursey visited Ev's mother, and Peter came for
her after school. "Ches is hoping we'll go into
the woods this Saturday, to find the sticks we

needs for the boat," he said as soon as he came in the kitchen door. "I got a small kettle. Nan could pack us a lunch and we could have a mug-up out on the barrens, if you wants to." The awkward shyness that kept them apart at school was gone.

"I'd like that," Ev said, even though she was uncertain what they were going to look for.

"Good," Peter said. "Maybe Doctor McCallum could bring you to our house on Saturday morning."

The next day, coming home after school, Ev passed her grandparents' house and went into Bannerman Park. She wasn't really allowed to do this but the park entrance was close to the house. If she hurried no one would notice she was a little late. Most of the park was open, but elms and maples grew near her grandparents' house. The sun slipped away behind the houses as Ev kicked around purposefully under the leaves, looking for wood that had been blown from the trees. Not sticks, but a limb big enough to give her the kind of wood she needed. Under her prodding, the sharp, sweet smell of dead leaves rose from the ground. After a few minutes, she found what she wanted. It was about the size of her arm, covered in smooth black bark and surprisingly heavy. She snapped the smaller branches off to make it easier to carry.

Now the hard part, Ev thought. She left the park carrying the wood, hoping no one would see her, especially not her grandmother. The short walk to the house passed without event. She slipped down the narrow lane between her grandparents' house and its neighbour, and left the wood beside the back steps where no one was likely to see it. Then she went around to the front door and entered as if she was coming home from school as usual. She knew there were some hand tools in the basement. Not many, but she had seen a small saw at least. Later, when no one was looking, she would go out and take the wood down there.

Chapter Seven

"Well, Ev maid, been busy with that knife of yours?" Ches Barrett was already in his fishing store when Peter and Ev arrived on Saturday. He spoke without looking up from his work.

"Yes I have," Ev said. From her coat pocket she extracted a bundle of sticks. She put them on the bench quickly, then thrust her hand back into her pocket. There, on the bench, were five of them, copies of the toy Ches had shown her how to make the week before, with five sticks to make the propellers turn. They were not perfect. The wood had unexpected knobs and waves that made it difficult to work. Ev held her breath while the old man slowly turned the silky white wood in his hands.

"This is hardwood, isn't it?" he said at last.

"Yes," Ev said, "I got it in Bannerman Park. From a limb blown off a tree. I sawed it and split it myself with tools I found in the basement.

These aren't as good as the first one I made," she added.

Ches looked at her with a twinkle in his pale blue eyes. "If you can do as good as this with hardwood, we may make a carpenter of you yet, my maid."

Ev smiled with relief. Peter picked up one of the toys. "This must have been some hard to do. Maple's twice as hard to carve as the spruce we uses here. Why'd you make so many?"

"I know someone with five little brothers and sisters," Ev said. "I thought I'd give them to her to mail home."

"Well," Ches said. "I thought today, before you goes off into the woods, I'd show you how to make a boat."

"A boat?" Ev couldn't believe it. She was sure it would take forever to win the old man's confidence. And how could he show her how to make a boat in just a few hours?

"Yes," Ches said. "A boat like this." He took a wooden toy from under the bench. It was a flat piece of wood, shaped into a prow at the front with a mast sticking up, something a little kid would use.

"Oh," was all Ev could say. She didn't want either of them to see her mistake.

But nothing seemed to escape Ches. "Don't be disappointed, Ev maid," he said. "'Tis only a toy, but wood is wood. Even toys can teach you the skills you needs."

So, while Peter began to work on the trap skiff, Ev sat and watched. Ches said almost nothing, letting his hands teach Ev as he worked. It was almost like watching a dance. Every movement did just what was needed with no waste of time or energy or wood. Watching, Ev realized how clumsy and unsure her efforts were, how much there was to learn.

Time seemed to stand still, so Ev could hardly believe it when Peter said, "It's almost one now. We got to move if we aim to get into the woods today."

"I'll show you the rest next week," Ches said, putting the pieces away. "Off you go now. Peter, I'll tidy up here."

Ev had been so absorbed watching Ches work that she had scarcely looked around. Now, going out the door, something carelessly left on the windowsill caught her eye. It was a flat, narrow piece of hardwood, less than a foot long, carved into an elegant shape. At one end, it came to a fine point like the prow of a slender boat. Just beneath this point it was hollowed in a clean U-shape that was divided by a sharp point of wood. It looked like the design for a cathedral window. Ev stopped so suddenly that Peter almost bumped into her. "Oh my," she said, "What is that?"

"Only a net needle," Peter replied. "We use 'em for mending nets. Come along now."

Ev left the store reluctantly, trying to commit the pattern of the net needle to memory. Here was something beautiful and useful. "Could I make one, do you think?" Ev asked.

Peter had already forgotten it. "A net needle? I

suppose, if Ches were to help you. Takes all day just to make one. They got to be made of hardwood, you see, to stand the pressure of the work. Softwood ones'll break in no time. We saves hardwood from old furniture just for that. A good one lasts for years though. Like an old friend, a good net needle is."

"Do you have one?" Ev asked.

Peter frowned. "No need now," he said. "My father got rid of them along with his other gear before he cleared out for Argentia. Come along now, Nan's packed a lunch for us," he said as they walked towards his house. He studied the grey sky. "I'm not sure I likes the look of the weather."

A few minutes later they were outside again. Ev managed to take the pack from Peter without hurting his pride and they walked along the narrow stretch of road leading from the Outer Battery. Ev drank in the salt air and looked down to the harbour, at the small fishing boats that were always there, and the bigger, dangerous-looking ships that spoke of the war.

"What are we supposed to do for Uncle Ches today?" she finally thought to ask.

"Well, remember I told you how we likes to use the green wood?"

Ev nodded.

"He wants us to find the sticks we needs. That's the lumber we finds in the woods," he explained. "If we wait to go looking there'll probably be a snowfall. Today we got to find the sticks and mark them for cutting later. It isn't just a matter of cutting down any tree. There's certain shapes to match certain parts of the vessel."

"What parts?" she asked.

"Well, the stem for one, the foremost part of the boat. For that you need a tree that grew bent, the way a heavy snowfall sometimes bends a tree when it's young so it grows with a curve to it. You understand?"

Ev nodded again. She knew exactly what Peter was talking about.

"Then, from the roots of a tree, you knows how the roots fork out? We'll find the right pieces for two other parts."

"What other parts?"

"Well, the stern knee for one, and. . . one part more." He stopped abruptly and blushed. Ev couldn't understand why.

"What part more?" she persisted.

He looked embarrassed, then looked down. "The breasthook," he mumbled.

"Oh." Ev felt the blood rushing to her own cheeks. I had to ask, she thought.

Peter quickly changed the subject. "We'll cut across Signal Hill to Quidi Vidi Village, then into the White Hills. That'll save some time. It's quite a hike. Are you up to it?" he asked her.

"My father and I traipsed through the woods all around Belbin's Cove, for miles and miles. I'm sure I can keep up with you," Ev said.

"Sure, that's nothing to brag about, Evelyn," Peter replied, laughing.

"I'm sorry. I didn't mean..."

"Never mind. I knows I'm slow. I knows there's things I can't do. It don't bother me to talk about, not with a friend."

"Peter, can I ask you something?"

"I suppose so," Peter said. Ev noticed the reluctance in his tone. He probably thinks I'm going to embarrass him again she thought.

"Uncle Ches knows you have a hard time getting around. Why did he ask you to do this and not someone else?"

Peter smiled. "Uncle Ches never seems to notice my leg," he said. "Never expects me to give in to it. Besides, he's teaching me to build boats, not anyone else. He can't ask just anyone to chose the proper sticks, you know."

The pride in his voice made Ev understand why Ches Barrett entrusted this work to Peter. "I wish he felt that way about me," she said.

Peter looked surprised. "You're right serious about learning all this, aren't you?"

She nodded. "It beats the hell out of letting Letty Winsor teach me how to choose the right shade of lipstick."

Peter laughed. "She's a hard case, that Letty Winsor. I'd steer clear of her if I was a girl."

"Well, I figured that out, finally."

They walked up a dirt road, past the last of the houses, to Signal Hill Road. Peter showed Ev a right of way that led through an old farm to the barrens of Signal Hill. The land was dotted with small ponds and boulders, and carpeted with plants that grew no higher than Ev's knee. The lower paths were boggy, and when they were a safe distance from the military base, Peter led the way to a dry path farther up the hill. It was colder than it had been last Saturday. The overcast sky hung low and even in the shelter of Signal Hill the wind had a chill to it, a taste of the long winter to come. Frost had touched blueberry bushes among the grey rocks, painting their leathery leaves bright crimson. Ev breathed the chill air deeply. Places like this felt like home.

She didn't really mind that Peter moved so slowly because it gave her plenty of time to look around. Ev enjoyed small details most people overlook, the patterns of grey-green lichen on the rocks, the insignificant plants that grew on the barrens. These she knew by the names her father had taught her: Lambkill, Labrador Tea, Bog Rosemary with its needle-like leaves. They were old friends. The land had a curious feel to it here, for it had been walked upon for hundreds of years without ever being home to a single human being. It seemed as if anything might happen in such a place.

As they walked, Ev told Peter about Belbin's Cove. He said very little. Ev wondered if she was talking too much, or talking about herself too much, or just boring Peter. He was so quiet it was hard to tell.

Then down the hill a ways, in a steep-sided valley, Ev noticed an odd collection of rocks. The arrangement was too careful to be natural; it was something once made by man.

"What is that down there, Peter?" she asked.

He stopped. "Where?" and when she pointed he replied. "That's the ruin of an old spring house. There's a well in there. They used to fetch water from there for the soldiers on Signal Hill, back in the old days."

"I thought they'd get their water from the ponds," Ev said.

"So they did too, but sometimes in the summer the water in the ponds gets bad. Then too. . . " he stopped and looked uncomfortable.

Remembering her embarrassment a short while before, Ev almost didn't press him. But this seemed different and she wanted to know. "Then too, what?" she asked.

"There's something about wells and springs that draws people," he said. "That could be why they put the spring house there. They're places where the earth and what's held secret under the earth meet."

"You sound like Uncle Ches when you talk like that." She laughed.

He laughed too. "Well, who else would tell me such a thing?"

"We have some time, right Peter?" she asked.

"We have all afternoon. Why?" He was more uneasy now.

"I'd like to go down and see that place. I know its a climb. You could stay here and wait."

"Ev, I'm supposed to look out for you. You shouldn't be going down there alone. There's an abandoned well inside."

"I won't fall in, silly. I'm careful. I just want to look."

Ev noticed the reluctance in Peter's eyes. He was silent for a long time. "All right," he said at last. "Just so's you don't stay too long." Then he fished into his pocket. "Here, take this with you." He held something out on the palm of his hand.

Ev looked at it, puzzled. It was a silver coin, a Newfoundland five cent piece. "What's that for?" she asked. She was about to make a joke, but something in Peter's face stopped her. She had never seen him look so serious.

"Luck," he said.

Ev waited for him to explain, but he remained silent. She shrugged and took it from him. It was smaller than a ten cent piece, almost weightless in her hand. "Sometimes you're an odd one, Peter Tilley," she said.

He nodded. "Sometimes I am. Now don't waste time down there. We still have work to do."

Ev moved down the slope quickly. Even though she hadn't minded walking so slowly with Peter, it felt good now to walk at her regular pace. She looked back once or twice and it seemed as if Peter hadn't taken his eyes from her. When she reached a small plateau, she waved.

She was out of his sight for a moment, skirting a boggy patch of land, when she heard it. Sweet, high music echoing out over the hills, the tune so sad and beautiful it almost made you forget who you were. It seemed to be coming from the ruin of the spring house. Maybe, she thought, if I'm quiet, I can see who's playing.

Peter sat on a rock and watched her travel down the steep incline, surefooted and graceful on the rocks. He cursed himself for not being able to go with her. Was it really his leg that was keeping him here, or was he being a coward, letting her go where he didn't dare? Perhaps he should have tried harder to stop her. There were stories about that place. . . but no, that was all foolishness. Foolish enough that you gave her the coin, he reminded himself.

Ten minutes passed, then twenty. The sky darkened and a cold, steady rain began to fall. Peter cursed. He'd be soaked to the skin after a while. Where was Ev? She'd promised to be quick. He stood and looked for her but there was no sign of life about the old spring house. Peter knew the rain made time slow, but at least ten more minutes passed. He tried calling for her, but he wasn't sure his voice would carry that far, not with the wind against him.

He was going to have to make the climb after all, and alone too. Peter left his pack beside the rock and cursed again as he began to climb down, silently saying things he'd never speak aloud. It really was too steep for him, and after a few minutes he was breathless with exertion. There were places where he could only drag himself down steep slopes and his cane was useless. Soon his clothes were covered in mud and his hands were grazed. I'll be in for trouble when Nan sees me like this, he thought.

It took so long. Another half hour passed before he was near the spring house. Almost an hour since she'd left him. Something must have happened to her, he thought. How could I have been so stupid as to let her come down here alone? He shouted her name as he approached the ruined building, trying to keep his voice calm and even. It couldn't be that something bad had happened to her, it couldn't.

The spring house still had four walls, though some were only a few feet high in places. It was roofless. He rounded the corner of half-broken wall. The doorway with its stone arch was still in place. He walked through.

Peter stopped dead. The ruin was completely empty. It looked as if no one had visited for months. The old well was covered with a large stone. Too large, he saw at once, for a young girl like Ev to move. He pushed against it with both hands, but it held firm. He let out his breath slowly, some of his fear abating. At least she hadn't fallen in. But when he circled the old building completely, there was still no sign of her. Where could she have gone? He'd barely taken his eyes off the place. It seemed impossible that she could go astray. He shouted her name again and again, trying to keep the edge of panic from his voice.

Finally, Peter knew he would have to return to the Battery to get up a search party. Surely this was just a bad dream and he would wake up, safe and dry in his own bed. He sat on a rock just outside the spring house to collect his thoughts for a moment and buried his head in his hands while the cold rain pelted down, soaking him to the skin.

Ev approached the spring house soundlessly, moving towards the music. She could not have stopped herself if she'd wanted to. Holding her breath, she made her way towards and through the old doorway. There she saw the man who was making the music. He was sitting near the well, playing a shiny tin whistle with his eyes shut. He seemed as entranced by the music as she was. He had coal black hair and although he looked like an adult, Ev noticed he was as small as a child. She stayed still listening, until the music stopped. When he opened his eyes and saw her, he jumped with fright. Ev thought he would have run away if she hadn't been standing in the only doorway.

It was so funny Ev had to laugh, although she knew that was probably rude. "I didn't mean to startle you," she said. "I'm sorry. It's just that the music was so lovely."

He looked at her for a long time before replying. His eyes were black as coal, almost as if they had no iris at all, and his face was curiously blank, without lines, without expression. Then he spoke in a soft, high-pitched singsong. "What brought you here, what brought you here? You shouldn't have come, you shouldn't have come." He seemed to be speaking to himself. He must be simple, she thought, or insane. He couldn't hurt me though. Or could he?

"It was the music. Such beautiful music," she said again.

"You caught me once, you caught me once. Now you belongs to me," he said.

Ev jumped when he spoke these words. But he's only some poor creature, she thought, and he's really too small to harm me. "I certainly don't belong to you," she said. "I just came here to look at the spring house, and now I'll be going back to my friend."

He looked at her with those curious black eyes and said, "We'll just see, just see, just see about that."

"Yes we will," Ev said. But when she began to turn she found she was stuck fast to the place where she stood.

The little man cackled, content to watch her struggle. Ev couldn't understand what was happening. "Please," she said after a moment, "Peter's waiting for me. I've got to go."

Then he spoke in a soft, wheedling voice. "You'd be better with me, better with me, better come with me." He hopped off his stone and came towards her. Ev realized he was even smaller than he'd seemed. He barely reached her waist.

"No!" Ev cried. She was trying hard not to show how frightened she was, but tears were beginning to sting her eyes.

"Oh yes, oh yes, oh yes," said the little man. He reached out to take her hand. As she drew it back, he snatched the other one. Ev's hand flew open to defend herself and he withdrew his quickly with a howl of pain.

Ev realized he'd touched the coin Peter had given her. She'd carried it in her palm the whole time without noticing. Now she held it up before her.

"Let me go," she said, her voice shaking, "Let me go or I'll. . . I'll place this right between your eyes."

That worked even better than Ev could have hoped. The little man drew back. "Treacherous, dangerous maid," he cried. "I could have kept you by my side. I could have shown you wonders. You catched me once. No one ever sees me twice. Catch me twice and I'll give you the thing you wants, your heart's desire."

But Ev barely heard his words, for at last she could move. She turned and ran as fast as she could from the roofless building, into a hard, cold rain. She almost stumbled over Peter who was sitting on a stone, his hands covering his head.

"Peter!" she cried. He was rain-soaked and his clothes were streaked with mud.

Peter raised his head, astonished. A moment before he had been alone. He stood and put his arms around her, pressing her to his wet jacket. He noticed two things: she did not resist his touch, nestling thankfully under his chin, and, although it had been raining for at least an hour, she was completely dry.

Chapter Eight

After a moment Ev looked up at Peter. "How did you get down here so quickly?" she asked. "A minute ago, you were 'way up the hill."

"Ev, it's been at least an hour since I saw you. Where on earth have you been?"

"No it hasn't. I was in the spring house, just like I said I'd be."

"But I was in the spring house. It was empty. Ev, there was no one there."

"Of course there was. I was there. How could you miss me?" Ev put her hand up to her forehead.

Peter glanced back apprehensively. "We've got to get clear of this place," he said, then he groaned.

"What's wrong?"

"The pack. I left it up the hill."

"I'll climb up there and get it," Ev said.

"No!" Peter shouted the word so loudly that

Ev was startled. "I was foolish enough to let you out of my sight once," he explained. "Besides, it's quicker to get home if we follows this valley out. Someone can come back for the pack later."

Ev noticed that Peter was beginning to shiver, so she followed him without arguing. As they walked, he seemed to be watching her. He even touched the sleeve of her coat from time to time.

"You're sure you're not hurt?" he asked several times.

Finally she lost patience. "Look, you're the one who's soaking wet and covered with mud. Remember? If I was hurt, you'd know it."

That certainly sounded like Ev.

As they approached the road, Peter and Ev saw a man in oilskins, waiting. Even from that distance, they recognized Ches Barrett.

Ches didn't even smile as they approached him. "Glad to see you don't need me as much as I'd supposed," was all he said.

When they opened the door to Peter's house a while later, Mrs. Bursey gave a cry of distress. By now, Peter and Ev were both soaked, but Peter had clearly had a harder time. He was pale and shivering. He was not scolded for the condition of his clothes as he had feared. Instead, Mrs. Bursey shooed him upstairs to change. "I'll make a pot of tea," she said.

While Peter changed, Ev hung their wet coats near the stove to dry. When he returned, they sat around the table, the older man and woman, the boy and girl, with steaming mugs of tea. Mrs. Bursey put a plate of bread on the table. Ev took some, suddenly realizing she had eaten nothing since breakfast. Peter, she noticed, ate nothing. Rain rattled against the windows with each gust of wind. Even in dry clothes in the warm kitchen, Peter was still shivering.

"Now, Ev," he said, "I wants you to tell us just what happened out there, then I'll tell what I knows and we'll see what sense Uncle Ches can make of this for us."

Ev looked at him for a moment, then shook her head. "It's the strangest thing. I can't remember. One minute I was walking into the spring house, the next, I ran out into the rain and you were there."

Peter looked amazed. "You can't recall? Ev, you ran from that place like a bat out of hell."

She shook her head again. "I'm sorry."

"Youngsters," Ches Barrett said, "tell me the tale from the beginning. You were going to look for the sticks we needs for the skiff. What happened after you left here?"

They told him how they'd crossed Signal Hill and how Ev had wanted to see the spring house.

"The spring house," Ches said quietly. "What happened, Ev my maid, after you left Peter? Think carefully."

"Well, I started down the hill and I remember thinking how nice it was to move so fast," she said with a guilty glance at Peter, "And then. . . music! I heard music." The memory of it made her smile, then frown. "That's as much as I can recall until I ran into Peter."

"And how did you feel then?" Ches asked.

"Afraid. Really frightened, but I don't remember why."

Then Peter told his half of the story. How he'd entered the empty spring house and tested the stone covering the well, and how he was about to return to get up a search party when Ev ran into him. "And that was the queerest thing of all," he ended. "It had been raining a good hour then, and I was almost soaked to the skin, but Ev was dry as could be. Hardly a drop of rain on her."

They sat silent for a moment, then Ches said, "Well now, youngsters, I think we've had enough excitement for one day. Let's say we phone Doctor McCallum and get Ev safely home."

"But Uncle Ches," Peter protested. "I thought you'd make sense of this for us. You must be able to tell us something." Ev could see how upset he was.

Ches shot him a stern look. "Peter, my son, I said it's time to get Ev home."

When Ev's grandfather came she put on her coat to leave, reached into the pocket and laughed. "Oh look," she said. "Here's that five cent piece you gave me, Peter. Do you want it back?"

"That's all right, you keep it," Peter said. Ev noticed the look he exchanged with Uncle Ches.

When the door closed behind them, Peter looked contrite. "Uncle Ches," he said.

"Yes?"

"I'm sorry we never got the sticks you needed."

Ches put a hand on Peter's shoulder. "Never

mind that my son. I'll have my son-in-law take us over the White Hills way in his truck some day. 'Tis his skiff we're building after all. Now, I wants to talk to you about Ev. You knows and I knows what happened out there today, my son. That maid was fairy-led if anyone ever was. But there's no sense in letting her know that if she can't recall." Peter started to speak, but Ches stopped him. "Now I won't say you should have stopped her from going into that spring house alone. She's some stubborn, that girl. No sense in blaming yourself for that. 'Tis a damned good thing you had the presence of mind to give her that five cent piece. I don't doubt but for that we'd all be out in the rain searching for her yet."

"But Uncle Ches," Peter said, "How do we know for certain it was Ev who came back? Perhaps she was changed. Or perhaps it'll make her simple, what happened."

"Is that what's been worrying you?" Ches asked and Peter nodded.

"Now that maid who sat at this table with us was Evelyn, I'm certain. You needn't fear that she was switched for. . . for one of them," he said.

Then Mrs. Bursey, who had only listened until now, spoke. "As for her going simple, Peter, well it seems to me that comes from the shock of it as much as the magic. As long as she can't recall what's happened to her, she'll be fine."

Ches nodded. "In any case, there's nothing weak about her mind, as you yourself knows. With a mind like hers, we shouldn't have to worry."

Only then did Peter stop shivering. But he still had questions. "How is it she could see. . . whatever it was and I couldn't?"

"Well, my son, there's some can see and some who can't. I couldn't tell you why. Some say it's all according to the time of day you were born, that those born between darkness and light have the gift while others don't. Then too, some say the time of day itself has to do with it. Some who can't see the fairies in the broad light of day can see them at sunrise or sunset."

"And where did she go, do you think, when I was in the spring house and it was empty? She said she was in there the whole time."

"Peter, my son, 'tis more than I can say."

"And where were you and Peter today?" Ev's grandfather asked. Safe in the big Packard, the windshield wipers beating out a sleepy rhythm, Ev wondered how to explain what had happened. It was better not to try.

"We were going to look for trees they need for the boat that's being built," she said. "But we went down a steep slope and Peter got all muddy and it started to rain, so we came home."

It all seemed like something that might have happened in a dream in any case. Perhaps it was.

They were almost home before Ev remembered her grandmother's vanity table and the angry scene in the kitchen the week before.

"Grandpa, I was just wondering . . ." she took a deep breath and continued. "Will Millie really have to give up some of her pay because of the vanity table? She works really hard and it doesn't seem fair."

"Your grandmother's bark is worse than her bite Ev," he said. "We talked it over and decided that would be unnecessary. You're right about Millie, she is a hard worker and she certainly didn't intend to hurt that table. There are lots of jobs for a girl like her these days, and we have to be good to her."

"Well, I'm really glad," Ev said.

"I didn't realize you and Millie were so close," her grandfather said.

"She's. . . she's been pretty nice to me." Ev felt her face burn, and was glad that her grand-father was busy watching the road.

"Well, I'm pleased to see you getting along. I've always felt that you can tell a lot about a person by watching how they treat someone they don't have to be nice to," he said.

In that case, Ev thought, it's a good thing you don't watch Grandmother.

Ev checked the mail when she came in. Still no letter from her father. In the kitchen, Millie was mooning over shoes and dresses and winter coats in the Saturday paper as usual.

Ev reached into her coat pocket. In spite of everything that had happened that afternoon, the toys were still there. She didn't know where to look as she put the sticks on the table. Suddenly, they seemed clumsy and silly. "These are for your brothers and sisters," she said, "I made them myself."

"Why Evelyn, that was right kind of you." Ev

was afraid Millie might laugh at her efforts, but there was only pleased surprise in her voice.

"Let me show you what they do," Ev said, and in a moment, they were laughing together as Millie tried to make one work.

"I'm sure they'll all be delighted," Millie said finally, putting the toys in her apron pocket. She hesitated a moment, then said, "I'll play cards with you after supper if you wants." Her tone was deliberately casual.

"But Millie, it's Saturday night. Don't you have a date?"

Millie shook her head. "You were right about Gerry, Evelyn," she said. "He's nothing but trouble. He wouldn't let me dance with anyone else, always thinking I had my eye on some other fellow. He...he wasn't kind to me. I told him last night I wouldn't be seeing him again. I'll not end up in the same boat as my mother, by God I will not," Millie said. Ev had never heard her talk like that before. Millie's eyes glittered with determination for a moment, then she smiled. "It'll take me a few days to take up with someone else. I'm in no great hurry."

So after supper Ev sat across from Millie at the kitchen table. Millie wanted to play gin, but Ev preferred cribbage, a game her father had taught her. She'd even found his old cribbage board. Ev won several games, they had some tea then played some more. It was about ten-thirty when Millie said, "You don't mind if we listens to the radio, do you? We'll just put it on quiet.

Lively music played out over the static on the

radio. Under the table, Millie's feet started doing little dance steps. "I loves this program. 'Uncle Tim's Barn Dance,' you know? They broadcasts live from the K of C Leave Centre, just down by your school."

Ev nodded. She knew the brand new building almost opposite her school on Harvey Road. There were almost always servicemen hanging around near it, and she was glad she walked home in the opposite direction. Millie sighed. "Gerry was always saying he'd take me to one of them broadcasts. Never did. Oh well. Tickets are some hard to come by."

"Millie," Ev said after they'd counted up their cards, "What are the dances like?"

"Oh, they're some fun Evelyn. Sometimes they have spot dances, you know, and you wins a prize if you're near the spot, and they have elimination dances, to pick the ones who dances the best. Gerry and I almost won once," she said, looking a little downcast again.

Ev wondered what it would be like to be older and go to a dance in a pretty dress, her hair swept up. Maybe one day Peter...but then she remembered. Peter wouldn't be dancing. Well, it was a silly thought anyway.

"Come on there Ev. You're somewhere else tonight," Millie said. "Thinking about that fellow of yours, are you?" Millie teased.

Ev surprised them both by blushing. Well, she had been thinking of Peter, hadn't she?

Both girls jumped a little when a knock came to the back door. It was so late. "Could be someone looking for the doctor," Millie said as if to reassure them both. But when she opened the door, it was Gerry.

Millie squared her shoulders. "Gerry," she said, "I told you last night I wasn't going to see you again. Now, you'd better be on your way."

Although he was partly in shadow, Ev could see the soldier's face from where she sat. He wore a curious, expressionless look. It reminded Ev of someone she'd seen somewhere, or maybe a dream she'd had. She couldn't recall.

"There's someone else, isn't there?" he said. His voice was low and intense.

"No, there isn't. I told you that before. There's nobody else. Now, you got to go." Millie tried to shut the door, but he grabbed her by the wrist and held her there.

"Millie, you belong to me."

From where Ev sat she could see Millie stiffen with anger. "I belongs," she said, "To no one but myself. Now let me go."

Ev saw Millie struggle to get away. She rose and stood behind her in the doorway.

"Let her go," she said, "Or I'll get my grandfather."

Gerry gave Ev a cold, steady look that made her heart pound, then slowly, deliberately he let go of Millie's wrist. She shut the door and locked it.

Millie was shaking. "I've got to get clear of him, that's for certain," she said, rubbing her wrist where he had held her. Ev could see red marks.

Cribbage wasn't much fun after that and Ev and Millie soon went to bed. But Ev lay awake for a long time, thinking. Millie was right to keep away from a man like that, a man who would use his strength and temper to get what he wanted. Her father and grandfather were not like that at all. Neither was Peter, and not just because of the weakness in his leg. Most people, she thought, would look at Gerry and Peter and say that Gerry is the better man. Most people are wrong.

Peter wasn't one for nightmares, but two or three times that night he woke, drenched with sweat, knowing he had dreamed of the spring house and those moments when it seemed Ev was lost. The last time it was almost dawn and he couldn't get back to sleep. He lifted the blackout blind beside his bed and lay looking through the window at the high rock cliff behind his house and the small patch of sky that was visible above. The rain had stopped in the night. It was that time of day when the sky is always grey. Would it be cloudy or blue, he wondered, when the sun came up?

Then he thought about Ev. He remembered how good she'd felt in his arms for that brief moment, the feel of her clean, soft hair against his cheek. He knew then if he stayed in bed his thoughts would take him where they shouldn't, so he swung his feet onto the cold linoleum and got dressed, quietly, so as not to wake his Nan.

He was about to make himself breakfast when he remembered the pack, left out all night in the rain. His first impulse was to leave it there, but that would be cowardly. Wasn't it his own fear that had put Ev into such danger to begin with? Besides, he couldn't afford to lose a perfectly good rucksack or the small kettle inside. In the tin breadbox near the stove he found a loaf of fresh bread his Nan had baked. He tore a chunk from it and stuffed it into his pocket, just as his Nan had all those years ago when he was a child. For luck, he thought. Then he pulled his coat on, took his cane and forced himself to retrace the path that he and Ev had taken.

He knew the land well and it wasn't difficult to find the rock where he'd left his pack. It was certainly worse for wear. The sun was coming up over the ocean by now, but here, in the lee of Signal Hill, everything was still in shadow. Suddenly, for no reason he could name, Peter's heart began to pound. He stood for a moment, trying to get a grip on his feelings. It was too much like the nightmares of the night before, too much like the fear he'd known as a small child. He felt trapped.

Then, against his will, his eyes began to travel down the steep hill, following the painful route he had taken in the rain the day before. He didn't seem to be able to stop himself. Serves you right, he thought, for being so fearful, for putting Ev in such danger. He broke into a sweat. But when he looked at the spring house there was no sign of anything unusual.

Somewhere a bird sang out. Peter sighed with relief.

"What in the name of God were you expecting?" he said out loud, smiling to himself. He

was about to turn away when he saw it; something small and dark, darting from a rock toward
the spring house. It might have been a rabbit or
his own imagination. He didn't wait to see if he
could tell. On the way home he vowed never to
go near the spring house again.

Chapter Nine

The weather turned colder, bringing snow and sometimes freezing rain. Ev hated to think of the house in Belbin's Cove sitting empty in winter. Somehow it made her chest ache to imagine the rooms all silent and cold.

Now everyone was thinking about Christmas. It didn't seem right to Ev that Christmas could come with everything turned upside down in the war and her family scattered like this. On Tuesday evening, Ev was sitting in the parlour with her grandparents while they both read the paper. That new Bing Crosby song that everyone was so crazy about, "White Christmas," was playing on the radio, forcing the holiday into Ev's thoughts while she pretended to read a library book.

"Look at this Ev," her grandfather said, "The Anglo-American Telegraph Company has special Christmas greetings for servicemen overseas for seventy cents. Perhaps you'd like to send one to your father."

He must have read my mind, Ev thought. "But Grandpa, how would it reach him?" she asked. "We don't even know exactly where he is."

"I'm sure it would find him. After all," he said, "Someone knows where he is. Come and have a look."

Ev did, seating herself on the arm of her grandfather's big plush armchair in a pool of yellow lamp light. The messages were all short. They said things like "Love and Best Wishes for Christmas and the New Year. All Well." Every one ended with "All Well."

"What do you think Ev?" he asked.

"I think that one would be fine," Ev said, pointing to one of the messages, hardly caring which. She hoped she sounded polite and grateful. She knew her grandfather was only trying to be kind, but she found the idea discouraging. "All Well." Was that what she would have told her father? She still wrote him every week, but somehow she never managed to say anything important. Those letters might not even reach him. It was like casting stones down a bottomless well.

If only I could tell him about Peter, she thought. I'm sure Dad would like him. I wish I could tell him what's happened to Mum, how she seems like someone who isn't there any more. But of course she could never say that. Just as she could never tell him how she missed home and how she missed him. "All Well" wasn't like anything she really wanted to say. Will he ever know? she wondered, a lump rising in her throat.

"I think I'll see what Millie's doing," she said. She quickly slid off the arm of the chair and went into the kitchen before anyone saw her face.

Millie was just finishing the pots, the dishes washed and dried and neatly put away. Usually, Millie noticed when Ev was sad. Tonight, though, she didn't even speak.

"Is something wrong Millie?" Ev asked after a moment.

Millie turned to her. "Well, perhaps there is, Evelyn."

"Why, what's the matter?"

"If I tells you, you got to promise not to say anything to anyone. All right?"

"Okay, if you want. Now tell me."

Millie frowned. "This morning, when I went to take the milk bottles in, I found this little package on the back stairs with my name on it. When I opened it, inside there was . . ." she stopped.

"What?" Ev asked.

"A dead bird. A sparrow. Somebody put it there for me to find."

"Oh, Millie. Why would anyone do something like that?"

"I'm not sure," Millie said.

"You think it might be Gerry?" Ev asked.

Millie nodded, biting her lip.

"Millie, don't you think we should tell Grandpa?" Ev already regretted the promise she'd just made.

"Oh no, we can't. If Doctor and Mrs.

McCallum thinks I'm the kind to cause trouble they might let me go." Now she looked as if she might cry.

"But Millie, you aren't the one who's causing trouble."

"Yes, but if I wasn't here, this wouldn't be happening at their house. Don't you see, Evelyn? I'm afraid of losing my place, especially since your grandmother is so, well, fussy about what people thinks and all."

Ev nodded. She was sure her grandparents would not replace Millie, but knew her grandmother could make Millie's life harder. She might even forbid Millie to go out in the evenings. Ev knew that Millie's social life was her one pleasure, but it was more than that. If Millie got married, she could get away from this dreary work, and Ev knew Millie was unlikely to meet a husband unless she was free to go out in the evenings. Ev could see why Millie wanted to keep her secret.

"Well, okay. I won't tell," Ev said. She could see Millie relax. "But you've got to tell me if anything else happens. Promise?"

The older girl nodded.

"Have you seen Gerry at all since last Saturday night?" Ev asked.

Millie looked evasive. "Not to talk to," she said.

Ev knew there was more. "But?"

"But, when I went out Monday and today, I did think someone was following me. Could be I'm wrong," she said, almost pleading for reassurance, it seemed to Ev. "Perhaps I'm just imagining things."

"When are you going out next?"

"There's a dance at the Caribou Hut tomorrow night. I'm going with Maisie Porter, you know, who works over to Mrs. Winsor's house on Circular Road? Only, I always walks over and gets her because Maisie's too timid to set foot out the door alone after dark."

Ev wondered what she could do. "Well, let me know when you're going," she said.

"Why?"

"Maybe I can watch from the window and see if anyone is around the house when you leave."

"Thank you Evelyn. I don't know what I'd do if you was one of them proper little girls, running to your grandmother with stories."

Ev laughed. "Not much chance of that."

After breakfast the next morning, Ev checked with Millie. No unpleasant surprises had been waiting with the milk that day. But Millie's problem lurked in Ev's mind at school. She wished she could talk to Peter about it, but they rarely spoke to each other at school. Although they'd never talked about it, they were both afraid of being teased. Peter might drop by for Mrs. Bursey at the house through the week. If not, Ev could tell him about Millie on Saturday.

That night, just before Millie left the house, Ev posted herself at the window of the darkened dining room, peeking through the blackout curtains. Luckily, her grandfather had been called away and the first floor of the house was deserted. This is silly, she told herself. What do I expect to see? But she saw him almost immediately: a man who slipped out of a lane across the street and began to walk after Millie when she left the house. There was no time to think. Praying that no one would see her, Ev flew into the vestibule, taking only her coat, and went out the front door just in time to see Millie turn and walk into Bannerman Park. The man had not yet reached the gate, but he seemed to be watching Millie. Ev stopped, amazed. She knew that Millie was going to a house on Circular Road, but couldn't believe she would be so careless as to go into the park alone at night.

Ev's grandparents' house stood with some others on an L-shaped piece of land that cut into a corner of Bannerman Park. There were entrances into the park at either end of the L. If I run, she thought, maybe I can get into the park from the other side and catch up with Millie. Then together we can ask this man if he's really following her and threaten to call the police.

Ev had never been out at night during the blackout. It was so dark. It wasn't difficult to run on the sidewalk but once she got into the park there were tree roots and slippery dead leaves to look out for. A sudden gust of wind blew some leaves into a high eddy beside her and she jumped. This part of the park had so many trees that it was easy for Ev to move without being seen, but it was so very dark. She shivered inside her old coat, wishing she had brought her hat and mittens.

Coming to the edge of the trees, Ev saw at

once she had badly miscalculated. Millie was far ahead of her, a shadow moving across the open part of the park. The man, who did appear to be following, was not close to Ev, but no farther away from Millie than she was. It would be harder for Ev to hide herself here. Just about the only shelter left was the brick band shell ahead. Without thinking much about it, Ev darted over and up the steps, into the band shell. She crouched down behind the waist-high walls, moving in the direction she'd last seen Millie. The leather soles of her shoes made ringing echoes when they met the concrete floor. She poked her head up cautiously. Millie was almost across the park now, perfectly safe. The man who had been following her was nowhere to be seen.

As she stood up, Ev breathed a sigh of relief. How silly she was, acting like she was one of those detectives in the serial radio programmes. Now she'd better get home before anyone noticed she was missing.

He was standing in the doorway of the band shell when she turned around, a tall man. Ev could have climbed the wall and jumped to the ground, but she froze.

"What brings you here?" he asked. It was too dark to be able to see his face. His voice was soft, not threatening.

Ev couldn't think what to say. She certainly couldn't tell him the truth. Even if this wasn't the man who had been following Millie, he'd laugh at her. She just said the first thing that popped into her head.

"Um. . . music," she said. "I like the band shell. It reminds me of the music they play in the park in the summer."

"You shouldn't be out here alone like this," he said moving towards her.

"You're right. I'll be going now, I just live over there." She pointed in the direction of her grand-parents' house, trying to keep her hand from trembling. Unless she was willing to turn and vault a wall, she would have to pass him to get out the door. She didn't want to do anything that might make her look silly. Besides, he was block-ing the doorway. She was almost beside him before she looked up into his face. It was Gerry.

"Not so fast," he said as she tried to pass him, and he reached out and grabbed her hand.

As soon as he touched her, Ev felt a panic rise inside of her. She was frightened of Gerry of course, but there was something else, another time and place something like this, a terror and danger she could almost recall. Her fear of embarrassment, the fear that would ordinarily have kept her silent, vanished and she screamed. It was like no sound she had ever heard herself make before. From inside the band shell, the scream resonated loudly out over the quiet night.

"Hey, what's wrong over there?" a young man's voice cried out somewhere in the park. It wasn't near, but Ev knew she was not alone. "Miss? Is something wrong?" the voice was getting closer.

Gerry looked at her before vaulting the wall of the band shell. His eyes glittered hard and black in the darkness. Then he was gone.

"Are you okay?" It was that voice again. Ev found it belonged to a young Canadian in an air force uniform. He was standing where Gerry had just a moment before, in the band shell doorway.

"Someone. . . someone tried to attack me," Ev said. That wasn't exactly true, but it seemed like the most reasonable way to explain what had happened.

"Well, gosh, you're just a kid," he said, coming towards her. Ev felt weak in the knees. She wasn't sure she could move.

"Are you okay?" he repeated. "Should we call the police?" His kindly face was puckered with worry.

"No, no, I'm fine. I've just got to get home, that's all."

"Well, you better let me walk you out of the park. A kid like you shouldn't be out here after dark like this. Don't your parents keep you in?"

"They don't know," Ev said thankful that she could at least tell him the truth about something. "I shouldn't be out."

"Well, you sure shouldn't. Betty," he called to a girl Ev hadn't noticed. "Betty, honey, come over here. Let's get this kid out of the park." The girl who came over was about Millie's age. She smiled shyly at Ev and attached herself to the airman's arm. They both walked Ev to the park gate, but she insisted on walking the half block to her own home alone.

Ev opened the front door quietly and put her coat in the vestibule closet. She opened the hall door to find her grandmother coming down the stairs. "Evelyn, what are you doing there," she asked, her voice sharp.

"I thought I'd lost a mitten," Ev lied. "I just found it."

"Well, I certainly hope you'd never try to go out alone. I just heard the most ungodly scream from the park. Shouldn't you be doing home work?"

"Yes Grandmother, I'll get to it right away." Ev made her way upstairs and collapsed on her bed, shaking. I have to see Millie in the morning, she thought. We have to talk.

That night, Ev dreamed she was in the band shell, or maybe it was the spring house on Signal Hill. It was a place that looked like neither, but somehow in her dream she knew it was both. And there was a threatening presence, someone who wanted to take her away. She struggled but couldn't move. His laughter echoed in her ears. Then somehow she could run, but she stumbled and fell into the open well, down, down, "You'll not catch me again," someone said as she fell. She awoke with a shock just before she hit bottom.

The dream stayed with her. Against all reason, she was certain Gerry was somewhere in the house and he would find her. Her heart beat loudly in her ears, blocking out all other sounds. After a few minutes she managed to get up and cross the hall into her mother's bedroom. The sound of her mother's slow, regular breathing calmed her at little. When she was small, her mother was always there to comfort her when she had nightmares. It would be so good to be little again, back in her parents' house where everything had been simple and safe.

She knew she should go back to her own bed now but she couldn't. Instead, she crept into her mother's bed. Good thing it was a double bed. Her mother was so big with the coming baby that she had to sleep on her side with a pillow to support her leg. Sleeping for two, Ev thought, and she smiled. Even without her father, there was nowhere as safe or as comfortable as her parents' bed. The terror of the dream was gone.

She managed to settle herself without squeaking the springs, but her mother shifted, opened her eyes and said in a sleepy voice, "Why Ev, what are you doing here?"

"I'm sorry, Mum, I had a nightmare. Do you want me to leave?"

"No, that's all right." She reached over and smoothed the hair off Ev's forehead, just as she had when Ev was a child. "You haven't come into our bed for so long. I thought you were too old to need me."

"No, Mum, I'm not too old. I wish. . ." she wanted to tell her mother just how much she did need her, but stopped herself.

"Wish what, my love?"

"I wish that none of this was happening."

"So do I," she said and she went back to sleep. Soon after, Ev fell asleep as well.

Chapter Ten

Ev woke when the alarm clock went off in her room across the hall and pulled herself reluctantly from the comforting warmth of her mother's bed. She was tired and last night's nightmare had settled like a weight on her chest. What had happened in the park seemed as distant and unreal as the nightmare itself. Ev wanted to talk to Millie, but she was so sleepy and slow to dress that there was barely time. After a hasty breakfast with her grandparents, she rushed into the kitchen.

Millie was singing a cheerful hymn while she washed the morning dishes. "He leadeth me, oh blessed thought, Oh words with heavenly comfort fraught. . ." she warbled.

How could she be so unconcerned! Then Ev remembered that Millie knew nothing about what had happened in the park.

"Millie" she said quickly, "You've got to keep

out of the park after dark. You shouldn't go out alone."

Millie didn't even ask why. "Oh, I won't Evelyn." She smiled one of those foggy, romantic smiles. "I met a new fellow at the dance last night. Raymond is his name, a Canadian serviceman from Nova Scotia. He's taking me out on Saturday night. Look," she said, holding up two tickets, "He got these tickets for 'Uncle Tim's Barn Dance' at the K of C Hall. Even gave them to me for safekeeping. He's some sweet Ev." And she went back to her dishes, humming.

Should I tell her? Ev thought. She seemed so sure that everything was going to be okay. It didn't seem right to upset her with what Ev knew about Gerry. Ev hesitated, then looked at the clock. She'd be late for school if she didn't hurry. "I've got to run," she said. "Maybe we can talk tonight."

When Ev saw Peter in the schoolyard that morning she wanted to talk to him, to ask him if he thought she should tell Millie or just let things be. But her shyness stopped her. Anyway, there were just two more days till Saturday. How much could happen in that time?

Still, Ev felt uneasy all day. When a knock came to the classroom door in the afternoon she jumped in her seat. Miss Smith read the note the secretary carried, then said, "Evelyn, you're wanted in the office of the headmistress." Somehow Ev was not surprised. There was just enough time to glance at Peter before she left the room. His nod steadied her. Ev followed the secretary down the stairs.

When the door to the office opened, Ev saw her grandfather. He stood up when she entered the room and, to Ev's surprise, put his arms around her and drew her close. He wasn't one for touching. Something terrible had happened.

"It's Daddy, isn't it?" she asked.

He nodded."Yes Ev, we had a telegram. He's missing in action in North Africa. That's all they can tell us for now."

The colour drained from Ev's face. Everything seemed to fade into the distance. "Sit down, Evelyn," her grandfather said, easing her into a chair.

"My dear," Miss Carlyle, the headmistress, spoke for the first time, "I'm truly sorry. Can we get you a cup of tea?"

Ev shook her head, forgetting even to say thank you.

"I'll take you home in a few minutes," her grandfather said.

"No," she whispered, then finding her voice, "No thank you Grandpa. I think I'd rather stay at school." The thought of going home, of facing her mother and grandmother in their grief, was more than she could bear. She was afraid her grandfather would tell her that her mother needed her, or that he might think she was being callous. But he seemed to understand.

"If you change your mind, I'm sure Miss Carlyle will allow you to leave whenever you wish."

The headmistress nodded.

"I should get back to class," Ev said and she

rose to leave. She wanted to kiss her grandfather before leaving him, but she couldn't. Suddenly she seemed to be encased in something as fragile as a soap bubble. Any wrong move or thought would break this thing and she would dissolve. Even the steps she took as she walked back up the stairs to her class were measured and careful.

When Ev stepped into her classroom she knew without looking that everyone's eyes were on her. Miss Smith must have told them. Ev kept her own eyes on her shoes as she made her way to her desk. She couldn't look anywhere else, especially not where Peter sat. She opened her workbook and began the arithmetic problems written on the board. Geography passed, then history. Sometimes she almost forgot. Then it came rushing back to her: he was missing; he might be dead.

The afternoon was almost over when the sudden, eerie wail of air raid sirens filled the air. Everyone began to stir. "Better not be those jeezely Huns," Ev heard one boy mutter.

"Remain calm," Miss Smith said. "I'm sure this is just a test or perhaps the sirens went off by accident. Now, move quietly out of the class, to the basement just as we've practised. Everyone line up at the door."

Ev's classmates obeyed, lining up two by two. From the corner of her eye, Ev saw that Peter was trying to get close to her. Sympathy was the last thing she wanted right now. Luckily, Peter was easy to outmanoeuvre. She quickly took her place in line beside Doris Piercy, who gave her a kindly glance. Ev looked away.

Everyone made their way downstairs quietly, Ev's class flowing into the others like a rivulet into a stream, until the whole school converged in the basement. There they sat on benches, waiting.

Waiting for what, Ev wondered. For the sirens to stop and the all-clear to sound? For the first bombs to fall? What difference does it make, really. If my father is lost, if he's dead, the war might as well come here. Let it sweep over Newfoundland and on to the rest of North America. Let everyone suffer like my father must have, like I am.

I loved him so much, she thought. How can it be that I'll never see him again? The sirens wailed on as if the whole city was venting Ev's grief. Against her will, one tear squeezed itself out, then another and another. Stop it, Ev told herself, stop it, but she couldn't. She put her head down, but that only made the tears fall into her lap. Her shoulders began to shake, as much with embarrassment and anger at herself as grief for her father. She felt Doris move away and someone else sit down. Ev expected an adult to speak to her, but no one did. She couldn't raise her head now and tears blurred her vision anyway, but somehow she knew it was Peter as surely as she knew the sound of his voice. He pressed a clean hanky into her hand then put his arm around her without saying any of the useless things she didn't want to hear. No one teased them or laughed. Not even Letty Winsor.

When Ev stopped crying she moved out from

Peter's arm, afraid of what the others might think even if they said nothing. She stayed close to him though. When the sirens finally stopped, the silence seemed loud in her ears. Then the all-clear sounded and the children began to chatter, but Headmistress Carlyle raised her hand for silence. "The afternoon is almost over," she said, "So, after returning to your classes, you might as well go home."

Peter and Ev went upstairs together. "I'd see you home," Peter said, "But I'd only slow you down."

"No, please, walk with me," Ev said, glad of anything that might keep her from her family a little longer.

When they finally reached her grandparents' house, Ev hesitated for a moment, wondering if she should take Peter in through the front door. Well, she thought angrily, he's my friend, not a servant. Then she realized that no one was likely to notice anything she did today.

The big house was hushed and tense inside. Even if you didn't know, Ev thought, you'd be able to tell something was wrong. Her grand-mother came into the hall. She had been crying and Ev felt a surprising sympathy at the sight of her red eyes. Whatever our differences, she thought, we both love him. Loved him.

Her grandmother came to Ev and hugged her. "My poor child," she said. "Those awful air raid sirens on top of everything else." She pressed her hanky to her face and began to cry again. "Whatever will we do without him?"

Ev groped for the right words. What were you supposed to say? "Now Grandmother," she said, "You mustn't give up hope." There, that sounded like something an adult would say. Anyway, Ev thought, you can't. I don't want you to.

"I know we'll never see him again," her grandmother said. She suddenly seemed so old and defeated. This isn't like her at all, Ev thought. She changed the subject, quickly turning to Peter.

"Grandmother," she said, "This is my friend Peter Tilley."

"I'm pleased to meet you Peter," Ev's grandmother said. She sounded as if she meant it. "Your grandmother has been here all afternoon with Ev's mother. She's been a great comfort. Perhaps you'd like a cup of tea in the kitchen," she added.

She wouldn't put him in the kitchen if he was a doctor's son, Ev thought, but she found she couldn't really be angry.

"Evelyn, I think your mother would like to see you."

Ev nodded and went upstairs. Thank heaven Mrs. Bursey is here, she thought. Even so it seemed as if her shoes were soled with lead. But when she reached the top of the stairs, Mrs. Bursey was standing in the hall with her hand on the door knob of Ev's mother's room. When she saw Ev, she put her finger to her lips, to make sure she didn't speak, and motioned for Ev to go back downstairs.

"I've just managed to get her off to sleep," she

whispered as they went down to the second floor. "Best thing for her at the moment. She's had a terrible shock. You should rest a while yourself if you'd like to."

Ev felt guilty about creeping up to her own room, but it was all she really wanted to do. She lay down on her bed in the gathering darkness, pulling the quilt up over her ears. Almost immediately, a deep, dreamless sleep carried her off to a place where there was no pain.

Chapter Eleven

When Ev woke the next morning, sunlight poured through the window into her eyes. The clock said ten-thirty. For a moment, she felt calm and rested. Then she realized it was only Friday. Why hadn't someone called her for school? As she sat up quickly in bed, the memory of the telegram flooded back to her. Her stomach growled and she realized she'd eaten nothing since yesterday noon. She rose and changed out of the school uniform she had slept in, then went into the hall. Her mother's closed door stood before her like a mountain, a stone wall, the hardest barrier she would ever cross in her life. Somehow, she made herself put her hand on the glass doorknob and push the door open.

Mrs. Bursey was already there. Ev's mother was sitting on the bed, her blonde hair neatly pinned back and although Ev could see she had been crying, she seemed perfectly calm.

"Ev, dear," she said when she saw her, "Come and sit with me," and she smiled. "She had a nightmare the night before last and she slept in my bed, Mrs. Bursey, just like a little girl. Can you imagine that?"

What's happened to her? Ev thought. Perhaps they haven't told her. Maybe, she thought with rising panic, she's gone mad.

"Your grandfather told you, didn't he Ev?" her mother asked. Ev nodded and tears came to her eyes.

"We can't give up hope, not yet. Your father may be safe somewhere. Perhaps he's been taken prisoner." She reached for Ev's hand. "I know I haven't been much of a mother to you since your father left. I want you to know that you can come to me now. Do you understand?"

Ev could only nod again.

Later, while she ate breakfast in the kitchen, Ev questioned Mrs. Bursey. "Why is Mum so calm? What's happened to her?"

"I've seen it before, child. A person's nerves seem stretched to breaking, then something like this happens and the shock snaps them out of it, brings them round to themselves again. Mind you, she's still very delicate and we must take good care of her. This may well hasten her time," she said, then noticing Ev's puzzled look, she explained. "Bring the baby on early I mean to say."

"What can I do?" Ev asked.

"Let her know you need her, just as you've needed her all along, my dear," Mrs. Bursey said. "Now that she's ready to be strong, she's got to have someone to be strong for."

That's something I can do, thought Ev.

The announcement appeared in the paper that day in the Casualty Report. "Missing in action," it said. "Duncan James McCallum, Newfoundland Artillery, in North Africa. Next of kin, wife, Nina McCallum of Belbin's Cove, Trinity Bay." It was the only item in the casualty report that day. Just underneath the announcement was something added to fill the space left by the deaths that had not happened. It said, "The albatross weighs less than 15 pounds, yet has a wingspread of almost twelve feet." Ev sat looking at the newspaper, reading those two items over and over, the one about her father and the senseless description of the albatross, trying to feel something. One meant about as much to her as the other did. It was as if her heart had been frozen or cut out.

She looked at the end table where her father's copy of *A Midsummer-Night's Dream* lay. She had not touched it since the day she first met Peter at the library, the day she went to the Battery for the first time. I stopped reading Dad's books, she thought. Did I do this to him?

There was no visit to the Battery that weekend of course. On Saturday, Ev's grandparents' house filled with people; doctors and their wives, people from church, grandmother's friends from the Women's Patriotic Association, and people Ev didn't recognize at all. For some reason, everyone brought food. The kitchen filled up with stews and pies, cakes and casseroles that no one wanted to eat. Millie was kept busy making tea and setting out plates of cakes and cookies. Ev helped her. Even with all the visitors, the house remained quiet and solemn. But it was not in Millie's nature to be serious for long and soon she was chatting away as usual.

"I likes that fellow of yours" she said to Ev after a while. "I gave him a cup of tea while he was waiting for Mrs. Bursey Thursday night."

"You never met Peter till then? He's been to the house before."

"No, I must have been upstairs looking after your mother. He's some handsome Ev. You never told me that. If only he didn't have that crippled leg."

"He gets along fine." The annoyance in Ev's voice surprised them both. "He's really clever. He's funny and he's kind. People look at Peter and all they see is someone who has trouble getting around. There's a lot more to him than his leg."

Millie looked down. "I'm sure that's true," she murmured and she said nothing more.

"I'm sorry Millie, I shouldn't have spoken to you like that."

"Never mind, Evelyn, it was my own fault for saying what I did. And your nerves is bound to be a bit strained."

Although Ev longed for peace and quiet, her grandmother kept calling her into the parlour to present her to strangers. Late in the morning, she was just about to sit down in the kitchen when Millie appeared in the doorway. "Your Nan wants you again," she said. Ev rolled her eyes and went into the parlour.

On the sofa sat Letty Winsor and her grandmother.

"Here's Evelyn," her grandmother said. She seemed more composed now, but tears were still close to the surface. "Say hello to Mrs. Winsor dear," she urged, as if Ev was a very small child.

Ev remembered Mrs. Winsor from the WPA. She was about the same age as Ev's grandmother, plump and dressed in a tight silk print. "My dear girl," she said, "I want you to know how very sorry we are. Your father was so brave and noble to go and fight when he could have stayed here. I'm sure his sacrifice will be remembered."

Letty said nothing but looked appropriately solemn. Like someone playing a part in a movie, Ev thought. I have to get out of here. "Would you like me to find Grandpa?" she asked her grandmother.

"Oh yes dear, if you would."

Ev stood in the hall, clenching and unclenching her hands. Hypocrites, she thought. When he went, they all thought it was wrong of him to leave us. Now he's some kind of saint. She took a deep breath, then knocked on the study door.

"Come in," her grandfather said. Of everyone in the family, he seemed the least upset by what had happened. He was sitting at his desk now, reading the big family Bible.

"Grandpa, I think Grandmother would like you to come into the parlour. More visitors."

He looked up, took off his wire-rimmed

glasses and put them carefully away in their case. Every movement spoke of calm and ease. "Aren't you coming Ev?" he asked.

"I think I've had all the visitors I can take just now," she said. One good thing about a crisis, she thought, you get to act strange.

"As you wish," he said and left the room.

How can he be so calm, Ev wondered. Doesn't he feel anything at all? She walked over to his desk and looked at the Bible. It was open to a chapter of II Samuel. Ev knew the story. King David's son Absalom rebelled against his father and was killed. Ev's glance fell on the last verse of the chapter her grandfather had been reading. "O my son Absalom," she read, "My son, my son Absalom! Would God I had died for thee."

She read the words over and over until her eyes filled with tears and she had to look away. Grandpa, she thought, I'm sorry. I didn't know.

When Peter came with Mrs. Bursey that afternoon, Millie left Ev alone in the kitchen with him.

"I'm being trotted out like some kind of trophy," Ev told him. "'I'm not sure how long it will be before I say something rude to one of these people. And it's all so queer. There isn't any funeral or memorial service, of course, because we don't know what's happened. I feel like time stopped when we got that telegram."

"But surely that's better than knowing that he's. . ."

"Dead? You don't have to be afraid to say it.

Yes, better, but not as real. Do you understand?"

"Perhaps I do. When you don't know, you can't get over it."

"That's right. As it is, I can't feel much of anything. Except. . ." she paused, unsure that she could say this, even to Peter. When she spoke again it was in a whisper. "Except I'm angry at him, for doing this to us. Everyone says he was so wonderful now, but they were right before. He had no right to leave my mother and me, to leave her expecting a baby." She hung her head. "I can't forgive him."

Peter paused for a moment. "When I was little and I first understood that my mother had died when I was born, I used to be angry at her for leaving me," he said.

"So I'm being pretty childish, right?"

"No. I think anyone would feel what you do now."

"Peter, why do you always know the right thing to say?"

He smiled. "I wouldn't say I do."

Ev thought for a minute. "But how did you stop feeling angry at her?"

"Well, I was just little you know. I made myself a story, see? And then I made myself believe it. It must have been cobbled together out of things I'd heard the grownups say. I told myself my mother hadn't gone to heaven to live with God, like they told me, but she'd been carted off against her will out on the barrens by. . ." Peter's voice trailed off. Ev couldn't understand why he'd stopped.

"By who?" she asked.

"By the fairies," he finished. Suddenly, he rose from the table and began to walk restlessly around the room. "I think perhaps I'd better go help Uncle Ches with that skiff after all. I feels right bad about leaving him to work alone. You don't mind, do you?"

Ev was surprised, but she shook her head. "Of course not. I'm fine here. Maybe next week I can come too," she said. Peter was out the door before she could say another word. Ev wondered what had gotten into him all of a sudden.

Later, Ev sat alone, grateful that the house was finally empty of visitors. When I talk to Peter, she thought, it doesn't hurt so much.

At supper that evening, Ev's grandmother pulled herself from her sorrow to talk of dressmakers and fabric. "On Monday I'll keep Evelyn home from school so she can visit my dressmaker. I don't suppose there's any point in you coming Nina. Your size will change so much when the baby is born after all."

Ev didn't understand what her grandmother was talking about, but her mother's head came up sharply, like a hunted animal. "You've never taken Ev to your dressmaker before, Mother," she said. "I see no need to now."

"But Nina, the child needs a proper black coat and dress. You can't mean to say that you'd let her be seen outside in her usual clothes now that this has happened."

Ev's mother put her napkin beside her plate and faced her mother-in-law. Her tone was careful and deliberate. "I'm sorry, Mother, but I mean to say exactly that. We do not know for certain that Duncan is dead, and I refuse to mourn him until we do. Ev has always hated black in any case. Even if. . . even if we learn the worst, I will not force my child to wear a colour she hates."

Everyone was speechless. Then Ev noticed tears welling in her grandmother's eyes. Her grandfather saw them too. "I think Nina is right, Gwen," he said, reaching across the table to take her hand. "No one expects us to mourn Duncan while there's still a chance he might be alive." Ev had never seen him take her hand like that before, or speak to her so gently.

Ev thought of all the times she had looked forward to seeing her grandmother put in her place. Now, instead of feeling happy, tears came to her own eyes. Why was everything so complicated?

After dinner, Ev dried the dishes for Millie. Anything to keep busy. But it had been a long day and both girls yawned when the water finally drained from the white porcelain sink. "Well," Millie said, "I think I'll get to bed early tonight."

"Tonight?" Ev said, "But Millie, it's Saturday. Weren't you going to 'Uncle Tim's Barn Dance' with that new fellow?"

Millie smiled. "It's sweet of you to remember that, Evelyn, what with all that's happened. Yes, I was, but I can't go off to some dance tonight. It wouldn't be proper. Ray phoned me Friday and I explained it to him. He didn't mind one bit. I promised to see him in a few days, when things quiet down."

Quiet, Ev thought, isn't really what's needed around here, but she nodded anyway. As she left the kitchen, she saw the two tickets for 'Uncle Tim's Barn Dance' sitting on the counter. What a shame, she thought. Millie wanted to go so badly. If it was me, I'd probably slip out after my work was done. No one would notice.

Ev had her Saturday night bath and shortly after fell into a heavy, dreamless sleep. But the night was not quiet. Several times she was dragged back almost to wakefulness. First, she heard a distant wail of fire engines, then the phone rang. Half awake, she heard her grandfather go downstairs a few minutes later. She was just falling back into sleep when she heard the motor of his car. Imagine Grandpa getting up in the middle of the night tonight, she thought sleepily. What could be that important?

Ev woke up Sunday morning with a burnt smell in her nose, the horrible odour of charred wood and singed wool. She remembered the sirens of the night before, the phone ringing and her grandfather's departure. She climbed out of bed, pulling her thick tartan housecoat around her, and lifted the blackout blind. The first snow had fallen in the night. The grey rocks of Signal Hill were dusted white. Everything looked peaceful, Christmas-like. Nothing's wrong, she told herself. At least, nothing new.

On Sundays, Ev was allowed to have breakfast in her nightgown and housecoat before changing into her Sunday clothes, an luxury unimaginable on weekdays. Padding down the stairs in her

corduroy slippers she noticed the burnt smell
again. It didn't get any worse as she walked
through the house, but it certainly didn't go
away. It wasn't burnt toast either.

No one was seated at the dining room table. It
wasn't even set for breakfast. Ev stopped, con-
fused. Breakfast should be on the go by now.
Then she heard voices in the kitchen. She pushed
through the swinging wooden door to find her
grandmother seated at the kitchen table. Oddly
enough so was Millie, and still in her housecoat
too! Whatever could be happening, Ev wondered.

"Sit down, Evelyn'" her grandmother said.
"We won't be going to church today. Something
happened last night just up the street. Something
terrible I'm afraid."

Ev didn't sit down. She stood there, trying to
make sense of things. "Was that why Grandpa
was called away in the middle of the night?" Ev
asked.

"Yes it was. Poor Ian. This on top of everything else." She fell silent, as if Ev was supposed
to know what had happened.

"It was a fire, wasn't it?" Ev guessed. It made
sense. The sirens, the burnt smell in the air.

Her grandmother nodded. "The K of C Leave
Centre," she said, "Burned to the ground. All
those people at the radio broadcast, trapped
inside. The windows boarded up, to meet the
blackout regulations. We still don't know how
many died. Perhaps a hundred, they say. Every
doctor in town was called out to treat survivors.

"I'm not sure when your grandfather will

come home, but I would like to be here when he does. In any case, the church is almost opposite the site of the fire. I couldn't bring myself to go there. Not today." She rose and left the kitchen.

Millie rose too, as if to shake off a bad dream, and went to the stove. "I'll get some breakfast started now. We'll all feel better when we've had something to eat." She glanced at the two tickets for 'Uncle Tim's Barn Dance,' still sitting on the kitchen counter. Millie turned to Ev and smiled wanly. "I was just telling your Nan about them tickets," she said. "It seems your father saved my life."

Chapter Twelve

It was snowing again when Ev went to school on Monday, hard pellets of snow that bounced and shattered as they hit the sidewalk. Rounding a bend, she saw that Harvey Road was roped off near her school. The road was covered with ice. It was thick, bumpy and a sickly grey; frozen water from the firehoses. Even at this distance, Ev could see crowds of people standing by the ropes, just looking towards the charred black hole where the new Leave Centre had been. There were firemen and police inside there, Ev knew, trying to make some sense of the fire, or worse, looking for the remains of those who died. Her grandfather had told them all about it when he finally returned to the house late Sunday afternoon, looking tired, pale and suddenly older.

"Sabotage. That's what people are saying," he'd told them, sitting in the parlour with a cup of tea in his hand. "Well, of course they would.

Even a fire in a shed looks like sabotage these days. It does seem strange though, from everything people told me. They couldn't stop talking about it, the ones who were lucky, the ones who survived. It happened so fast. One minute everything was fine, then the whole place was in flames. It was horrible, what they told me." And he fell silent.

Just for a moment, looking down the road, Ev could see flames against the black night, hear the screams of people trapped inside.

She made herself look away, then turned back towards Garrison Hill, taking the long route to school, away from the charred ruins.

Peter was waiting for her in the schoolyard. Ev stopped when she saw him, suddenly shy, but he came over. "Peter," she said, "Aren't you afraid you'll be teased if you spend too much time with me?"

"I don't give a. . . care what anyone says," Peter replied. "You're my best friend Evelyn McCallum. I don't mind who knows that."

At recess, Ev went out into the schoolyard, hoping everyone but Peter might leave her alone. But the first person she met was the last person she wanted to see.

"I. . . I was hoping to talk to you at your house on Saturday Ev," Letty said, "I wanted to say that I'm really sorry about your Dad."

Ev looked at her. The tears in Letty's eyes were not Hollywood movie tears. Ev thought of all the mean things she might say to Letty.

Suddenly, they weren't worth saying. "Thank you, Letty," she said and it seemed, even to Ev, as if she meant it. Then Doris came over and insisted Ev join them.

Everyone was talking about the fire. Ev was almost glad. It made her own troubles seem more distant, like something that happened long ago. There were so many stories about narrow escapes and daring rescues. Ev found herself telling Millie's story, ending with the part when Millie said, "It seems your father saved my life." Ev was asked to repeat the story several times over the day and everyone who heard it was impressed.

Suddenly lots of people wanted to be Ev's friend. But not everyone. Some avoided her as if bad luck might somehow be catching. But at the gym, girls fought to see who would be her partner. By the end of the day, Ev was worn out from all the attention.

"You know," she told Peter as they walked home from school, "A few weeks ago I would have been happy to have some of these girls as friends. Now I just wish they'd leave me alone. It's as if I'm war effort work. I don't want to be Poor-Evelyn-who-lost-her-father-in-the-war."

Peter nodded. "People thinks they're doing you a favour, giving you all that pity. But pity is some hard to bear. How's your mother getting on?"

"She's her old self again. It's hard to believe. But Grandmother's like someone who's had all the wind knocked out of her sails."

When Ev got home, Millie was waiting by the door. She gave Ev a funny look. "Your Mom wants to see you, right away," she said.

What now? Ev thought.

Her mother was sitting up in bed, knitting a little white sweater. She put the knitting down and gave Ev another curious look. "Sit down dear," she said. When Ev did, her mother reached into the bedside table. Then she held out an envelope. "This came for you today."

As Ev took the letter her hands shook so hard she could barely open the envelope. "From Dad," she said. "Then he's safe." She let out a breath she hadn't even known she was holding. Everything was okay.

Her mother spoke gently. "Ev," she said, "Think about it. This letter took weeks to reach here. The telegram travelled much quicker. Your father wrote this before."

"Oh."

"Perhaps you'd like to take it to your own room and read it."

"Don't you want to read it too?"

"After. He wrote to you, love."

Ev nodded and crossed the hall into her own room. She sat on the bed for a moment, barely daring to look at the letter. It seemed to reproach her for the anger she had felt over the past four days. When she opened it, she saw it wasn't much of a letter, really, just a note. Her father's handwriting looked hurried. She took a deep breath and began to read:

November 9, 1942

Dear Ev,

I know it's been a while since you've heard from me. I guess you think I've forgotten you by now. Not a hope. I think about you and your mother every minute of every day, and I wonder how you're getting on without me. I suppose you've turned into a city girl and you won't want to come back to Belbin's Cove, or wherever else we move next. But then, I really can't imagine you changing.

Now that I'm facing real combat, I think this wasn't the best idea I ever had. I'd give anything to be safe at home with you both again. I just want you to know that.

I'm doing my best to see that will happen. Tell your mother I'll write her first chance I get. It isn't always easy.

I love you both.

and it was signed, Dad.

One flat, round tear fell on the letter, smudging the ink. It's okay, she thought, you were just trying to do what was right. I love you. She put her head down on the pillow and cried and cried. She tried to be quiet, but her mother heard. After a few minutes there was a knock on the door.

"Are you all right, Ev? Do you want to be left alone?"

"You can come in." She choked out the words.

Her mother sat on the bed beside her and stroked her head while she cried. She wanted to stop for her mother's sake, but couldn't.

"Just go ahead and cry," her mother said. "You've been holding everything inside too much. It will do you good."

She was right. When Ev finally stopped, she felt lighter, as if the uncried tears had been weighing her down. She gave the letter to her mother, who slipped it into her pocket. "I'll give it back to you later," she said. Her mother's eyes were bright with tears too, but she wasn't crying. They sat together for a while without speaking. Then Ev said, "Mum, can I ask you something?"

"Yes, anything at all. I've been waiting for some questions from you."

"If Dad doesn't come back, what will become of us?"

"I've given that a lot of thought over the past few days. I'm glad you asked, because I want to know what you would like us to do." Her mother hesitated. "Of course, we could always stay here, if that's what you want," she began. "I'm sure your grandparents would like us to. . ."

"But Mum, that isn't what you want, is it?" Ev asked.

Her mother sighed. "Well, your grandparents have been very kind to us, but perhaps we should live on our own. That won't happen overnight though Ev. I'll need help with the new baby. Then I'll have to do whatever's necessary to bring my nursing certificate up to date. And I'll have to learn how to drive." Her mother's nose wrinkled. She never had liked the idea of driving. "We will be here for at least another year."

"And then?"

"We own the house in Belbin's Cove. Your father was always very careful about such things, and. . . there will be some money. Not a lot, but enough that I'll be able to hire a girl to live with us and take care of the baby. I'll apply for a job at the cottage hospital in Old Perlican, or maybe as a district nurse. In any case, I'm sure I can support my family.

"But Ev, people aren't going to like this. Women don't simply leave their children and go off to work, you know that as well as I do. The government may not even want to hire me, although, considering what your father did for them I doubt they will be able to refuse. We'll have a fight on our hands." She sighed. "And we must be very careful not to hurt your grandparents' feelings. I can support you and the baby, but if you are to have a good education, I'll need their help. I won't mind begging for that." She looked discouraged.

"Mum, I'll do anything you tell me to," Ev promised.

"Good. Now first you have to promise not to talk to your grandparents about this." Ev began to protest but her mother raised her hand to silence her. "Not a peep until after the baby is born. We've been through enough in the past few days. The baby's due in just a few weeks, and I have to save my strength for that particular battle. Afterwards, when I've recovered myself, we can begin to talk to your grandparents about our plans. Besides, we may learn that your father is safe in the meantime and all that fuss would have been for nothing."

"You're right," Ev said. "I'll do the best I can not to fuss, Mum, I have all along, ever since I promised Dad. . ." Ev stopped in confusion. The words had just slipped out.

"Promised Dad what?" her mother asked.

"You weren't supposed to know," Ev said, but the whole story came tumbling out: how her father had made her promise not to cause trouble when they moved to St. John's, the knife, the vanity table, everything.

When Ev finished, her mother looked grave. Ev expected her to be angry. After all, breaking grandmother's vanity table, letting Millie take the blame, these were serious things. But when her mother spoke there was no anger in her voice. "Oh, Ev, I wish he'd told me. I love your father, but he was mistaken. I thought you weren't coming to me because you didn't need me any more. That was one of the things that made me so sad. Now, you must make me a promise. Whenever anything is troubling you, you have to come to me. Promise?"

Ev smiled. She started to say "cross my heart, hope to die," but stopped herself. "Promise," she said instead.

"Oh, goodness!" her mother gasped, "This baby's a real kicker. Here, give me your hand." She took Ev's hand and laid it on the round of her belly. Ev was surprised by how it felt, not soft like flesh, but hard and round as a bowl. Then she felt something else. A small ball moved past her hand. She was so startled she drew her hand away.

"What was that?"

Her mother laughed. "A heel. This one's going to be a football player, boy or girl. All day long those little round heels move over the place. We have to think about names, you know. Your father and I never even discussed that."

"Achilles!" Ev said. "For the heels."

Her mother laughed. "I don't think so."

Ev looked more serious. "Duncan?"

Her mother shook her head. "No Ev, we already have a Duncan in the family. Anyway, why only boy's names? Maybe this is sister."

"Eleanor is a nice name."

"Yes, it is. I've always liked it. Suppose we agree on Eleanor a girl, and we'll talk boys' names over." She paused for a moment "Ev," she said.

"Yes Mum?"

"I guess you've wondered how I feel about this baby. All those weeks and weeks when I did nothing but lie around feeling sorry for myself, you may have thought I didn't want it."

"Well. . ." Ev found it difficult to lie, so she said nothing.

"I thought as much. I haven't been very happy. That's an understatement, isn't it? I've been miserable. I should have been better than that for your sake alone. I gave in to despair, which was wrong. It was partly because I knew I could, because I knew you were taken care of. But I was worried about the baby too. You know how many times I've tried. Three others. I was afraid to believe this one might make it. But now that it's so close, well, I always wanted another child. It used to hurt when you asked me why I wouldn't let you have a little brother or sister."

"Oh, I'm sorry."

Her mother laughed. "No, it wasn't your fault. It's just that now I can believe I'll finally be able to give you one."

When she turned out the lights that night, Ev raised the blind. In the darkness of the blackout she could see thousands of stars. Somehow even they looked cold on this cold night, glittering green against the black velvet of the sky. As Ev pulled the blind down she thought of Belbin's Cove in winter, the long blue shadows of spruce trees the moonlight cast on the snow, the distant ringing of sleighbells and laughter over the frozen night air. Maybe next year she would see these stars from her own house again. Nothing will ever be as easy as it was before, she thought as she climbed into bed. Nothing will ever be the same. But at least now I have my mother.

In her dream that night, Ev stood inside ruined walls of stone. She couldn't move. She opened her mouth to scream but nothing came out. A little man with black eyes and black hair grabbed for her hand. She heard him cry out, then she heard him say, "Catch me twice and I'll give you the thing you wants, your heart's desire." Suddenly she could move. She ran from the place and stumbled to Peter, but as soon as she touched his jacket he faded away to nothing. She was left alone in the cold, hard rain knowing she would never see him again.

Ev woke with a start. Peter, she thought. Peter, come back. Then she realized it wasn't Peter she'd lost at all, but her father.

Then she remembered.

It was as if she'd stumbled through a wall to find herself on other side. This wasn't just a dream. The little man, his promise give her the thing she desired, that had happened. She sat up bed, trying to think. I must be going crazy, she told herself.

But no. It was true. "My father," she whispered. "Give me my father."

Chapter Thirteen

When Peter and Ev walked home together after school the next day the sun had already dipped beneath the bare black branches of the trees. Blackout was only an hour away. They walked along Harvey Road in silence. Peter was always content to wait for Ev to speak, knowing she would. He was right. As they passed The Nickel, she turned to him and said, "I have some secrets to tell you Peter."

She looked so serious he had to smile. "That sounds mysterious."

"I'm serious. You won't tell anyone anything will you?"

"I'm not sure I can promise that, but your secrets are safe with me, you knows as much."

"Well, no one knows this yet, and I'm not supposed to talk about it, but Mum and I have been making plans about what we'll to do if. . .

if Dad doesn't come home. What do you think will happen?"

"I supposed you'd stay here with your grandparents." Peter said, wondering where this sudden sinking feeling came from.

Ev smiled. "I guess a lot of people think that. Well, we won't. My mother's got more spirit than that. No matter what happens now, we're going to go home."

Peter stood and listened while Ev told him about their plans, a smile fixed on his face. He was remembering the day his father had sold the fishing gear, how he'd stood there, watching the life he'd wanted being carried away in bits and pieces, not being able to stop what was happening. He felt like that now. Suddenly he realized Ev had stopped talking and was waiting for him to say something.

"Well," she prompted, "Don't you think that's great?"

The part of the road where they were walking had a clear view of the Narrows. Peter glanced out to sea as if to comfort himself. "Look," he said. "A ship's coming in." It was, too. It gave him a chance to turn away from her.

"Peter, this is what I really wanted. Aren't you happy for me?" Ev asked.

"Of course I am," he said. He wondered if the words sounded as flat and hollow as they felt.

Ev pressed on. "Let's keep walking. There's something else. Remember when I went into the spring house and you couldn't find me?"

"That isn't something I'd be likely to forget."

"Well, last night I had a dream and I remembered what happened."

This time Peter was too shocked to reply. He reached out and put his hand on her shoulder. The concern in his face surprised Ev.

"You knew, didn't you?" she asked. "You knew and you didn't tell me."

The disappointment in her voice stung him. It was like being caught in a lie. "I didn't really know, Ev, but I guessed you'd been fairy-led. It was the spring house, you see. I told you it was a place for secrets. I tried to stop you from going there, but I couldn't tell you why. I didn't really know you then. I was afraid you'd laugh at me."

"Well, I suppose I might have."

"I should have gone with you," Peter said.

"No, it really was too hard a climb."

He smiled. "Well, I found that out. And after, when we spoke to Uncle Ches, he wouldn't tell you what he knew. He said it would be better not to, as long as you didn't remember."

Peter's old fear had returned like an unwanted friend. He didn't want to know, but he couldn't stop himself from asking. "Just what do you remember, Ev?"

"I don't know if you'll believe me. There was a little man with black hair and black eyes. I couldn't move. He wanted to take me away, but when he touched the five cent piece you'd given me it drove him off. Then I could run. That's when I found you. But Peter, there's something else."

"What else?"

"He said if I ever saw him again he'd give me

my heart's desire. That's just what he said." Ev's eyes were bright with excitement. "Peter, don't you see what that means?" The exasperation in her voice was plain. "I might be able to make my father safe. I want to go to the spring house again. I want to try to find him."

"No!" Peter's voice was so loud that two servicemen walking across the road turned to look at them. "I'm sorry. I didn't mean to yell at you. But Ev, this is pure foolishness."

"You don't believe me," she said, that disappointment in her voice again.

"Yes I do believe you. That's why you've got to stay clear of that place."

"I don't understand."

"Say this little fellow really is. . . one of them. He tried to make away with you, didn't he? Why would he tell the truth? I never heard of fairies granting no wishes, not outside of fairy stories in books for youngsters, and you knows there's not a word of truth in them." He looked at her seriously. "Ev, these aren't just mild creatures, flitting round the barrens granting wishes. They're evil, soulless things. They wants to harm those with souls like you and me."

She gave him a look of scorn and pity. "Do you think I'd let myself be frightened out of trying to save my father?"

He sighed. "I don't suppose you would."

They walked on in silence for a moment. "Peter," Ev said, "I hoped you'd come with me."

Peter stopped again. He felt as cold as he had that day on Signal Hill.

"You will, won't you?" she persisted.

He wanted to say yes, but couldn't. "I don't know." That was as close as he could get. "Will you do one thing for me though?"

"What?"

"Come with me to talk with Uncle Ches." Peter felt sure the old man would be able to talk Ev out of this wild plan.

"Why?"

"He might know something that will keep you safe," he said. It wasn't really a lie. He might.

"Okay, but when? I can't wait until Saturday. I've got to figure out a way to get back there soon."

"I'll ask my Nan to have you over to the house for supper tomorrow night. Do you think you'd be allowed?"

"As long as Grandpa can come and get me I will. Peter. . . I'd. . . I'd really like for you to come with me."

Again Peter tried to say yes. The word just stuck in his throat. "I know you would," he said. He found he couldn't meet her eyes. The rest of the walk passed in silence. At the McCallum house, Peter found his Nan. Dr. McCallum had been called away, so they walked to the streetcar stop together. He hated to leave Ev disappointed like that, but there wasn't anything else to do.

On the streetcar Peter tried to sort out his feelings. Ev had just asked him to do what? Risk his life? Certainly face the thing he feared most. But she didn't even care enough to think how he'd feel if she went away.

Was it foolishness, this idea of saving her father? Maybe the memory of what happened out there on Signal Hill had unsettled her. Perhaps she'd go out and look and nothing would happen. That would be the best thing. No, it wouldn't. Saving her father would be the best thing, but how likely was that? And this. . . this fellow (he couldn't bring himself to use the word) if he'd tried to harm her once, what would he do the next time? There's nothing for it, he thought. We got to talk to old Ches.

"You're some quiet tonight, Peter my son," Mrs. Bursey said. Peter looked over and realized she had probably been watching him for some time.

"Well, I was just thinking about Evelyn, wondering what will become of her mother and her now that all this has happened."

"Well, this is a secret, but Nina McCallum told me today that they'll probably return to Belbin's Cove after a while." Peter knew his grandmother could read his expressions like a book. He tried to keep his face perfectly still. It didn't work. "I knows what you're thinking, my son," Mrs. Bursey said. Then she surprised him. "I'm not sure it will be the best thing for either of them myself. But that will sort itself out in time."

Peter knew his Nan had unfailing faith in the idea that things worked out for the best. He wasn't so sure.

"Now," his Nan continued, "I got some other news today. This one's a secret too. You got to promise to tell no one, though, especially not

Evelyn McCallum." She looked pleased and mysterious.

"All right," Peter agreed.

"Doctor McCallum took me aside before he was called away today. It seems there's a plan to set up a scholarship fund in Duncan McCallum's name to send a youngster away to Montreal to study engineering at the university there. One every year. He thinks it's too early to tell the rest of the family just yet, but people from the school board have been speaking with him." She looked so happy. Peter couldn't understand why.

"Well, that's nice I suppose," he said to be polite.

"Nice! Is that the best you can do? Don't you see why he told me? You keeps to your books and you might very well be one of the ones they sends. Doctor McCallum knows that as well as I do."

Peter nodded. He couldn't think of anything to say. The end of high school was years away, and there was so much else to worry about just now.

After Peter and Mrs. Bursey left, Ev came into the kitchen to find Millie sitting at the table, not working or reading the paper, just sitting. Millie never sat still this time of the day until supper was on the stove.

"Millie," she said, "Is everything okay?"

The older girl started at the sound of her voice. "Oh Evelyn, you gave me a turn. Yes, everything is fine, I suppose. Gerry was here today." Her voice sounded odd, as if it came from far away.

"Gerry? Again? Oh Millie, maybe it's time to get the police." Ev was about to tell Millie what had happened that night in the park, but Millie spoke before she could.

"No, everything will be fine now. He came to tell me he was leaving. This time tomorrow he'll be on a ship headed overseas. He came to ask if I would write to him. Just imagine that. After everything he did to me. It seemed as if he had no idea how I might feel, as if my feelings weren't supposed to matter." She stood up and went to the counter, spreading out newspaper to peel potatoes on. "I told him no," she said quietly. "I feels right bad, too."

"But Millie, why would you? He tried to make you miserable."

"Well, after all Evelyn, he could be going to his death over there." She glanced at Ev when she realized what she'd said, but Ev only nodded. She was right. "Still I never have been sure he wasn't following me, even till today. I'm going to be a lot more careful who I goes out with now. A man like that could ruin your life. Oh, look at that," she added, looking under the counter. "Out of potatoes again. There's a bag in the basement. Would you bring some up for me?"

Ev nodded and went towards the basement door, which was just opposite the back door. With her hand on the doorknob, she glanced out the window and froze. Gerry was standing near the garage. For just a second, his eyes met Ev's. Her heart pounded loudly. She had never seen such a look of pure hatred. She quickly checked the deadbolt on the back door. It was locked. When she looked out the window again, Gerry was gone. She flipped the light switch, bolted down the basement stairs and back up again as if someone was chasing her, and arrived at the counter with an armful of potatoes, panting for breath.

Millie looked at her, puzzled. "I didn't need them so quick," she said.

"That's okay," Ev panted. When Millie's back was turned, she looked out the window again. Gerry seemed to be gone. And tomorrow he would be gone, probably forever. If he wasn't, Ev thought, I'd go to the police or tell Grandpa. But I don't need to now. He's leaving.

When the phone rang just as everyone was sitting down for supper, they all groaned a little. Dr. McCallum was often called away at meal time and the hospitals were still busy with victims of the fire. "I might as well get that," Ev's grandfather said. Ev listened from the table as he answered the phone in the hall.

"Why hello, Mrs. Bursey. What can I do for you? Yes, I'm sure she can come to supper tomorrow. Oh, there's no need to ask her, she'll be delighted. I'll give her taxi fare just in case I'm called away. Otherwise she can phone me. I'll let her know what time she's expected to be home."

"Well," he said when he sat down, "That was a much nicer call than I expected. Evelyn, Mrs. Bursey has invited you to supper at her house tomorrow night. She said you can come home with Peter. I don't suppose you've been to the Battery since. . . since we had the telegram, have you?"

"No, I haven't," Ev said. It would only be a week tomorrow since the telegram had come. It seemed like a lifetime. Everyone sat silent for a moment, and Ev guessed they were all thinking the same thing.

Her grandfather broke the silence. "I had a chat with Miss Carlyle a few days ago. She told me Peter Tilley is making good progress with his school work. That boy could be headed for a scholarship from what I hear."

"Why were you talking to Headmistress, Grandpa?" Ev asked.

"Oh, I run into all kinds of people at the hospital you know. Visiting friends and all," her grandfather replied, but for some reason, he looked uncomfortable. If it was anyone else, Ev would have thought he was lying. But that couldn't be. Grandpa never lied.

That night in bed, Ev thought about Gerry. He wouldn't cause any more trouble now. I'm glad I didn't tell Millie about the night in the park, Ev thought.

Then she thought about Peter. He hadn't said he would come to the spring house with her. She thought for sure he would. Well, she thought, maybe Ches Barrett can help me talk him into it. What happens after that is anyone's guess, she thought as she turned out the light.

Chapter Fourteen

Peter and Ev came into the Tilley house just before dark the next evening, laughing together.

"Ummm, fresh bread, oh that smells lovely. Can I do anything to help with supper?" Ev asked.

"I suppose you knows how to peel turnips?" Mrs. Bursey said.

Ev nodded. Mrs. Bursey handed her the knife and put some turnips in front of her. It was time to turn on the lamp. Peter walked to the windows and pulled the blackout blinds down, leaving them all in darkness for a moment until the lamplight filled the room. "It's after getting dark some early. Soon be the darkest day of the year," he said.

"Just look at the size of the turnips this year," Ev said. "I read in the paper they lowered the grades so they could sell smaller ones than usual."

Peter had never thought of Ev as the sort who could keep up her end of a conversation about turnips. He had to smile.

"Even at that," Mrs. Bursey said, "I hear they fined some shop keepers for selling such poor ones. No turnips from Canada this fall is the problem. The war. Changes everything, don't it?" she said and Ev agreed.

At supper, Ev praised Mrs. Bursey's cooking and asked questions about her work as a midwife. There were things that couldn't be discussed in front of Peter, of course, but she seemed happy enough to tell Ev her stories of almost getting lost in a snowstorm, and of a rough trip in a small boat across the harbour to help a woman who was having twins. "They made me Godmother to those babies. I'm Godmother to over twenty children," she said, a note of pride in her voice, "Twenty-three."

After Peter and Ev finished doing the dishes, two women came to chat with Mrs. Bursey. They glanced uncomfortably at Peter and Ev. Peter saw his chance. "Nan, I thought we'd take a walk over to Uncle Ches's. Let Ev see how the skiff is coming on."

"Just remember tomorrow's a school day," Mrs. Bursey said as Peter and Ev scooted out the door.

A small curl of smoke rose from the chimney of the Barrett house. It was dark and cold inside. Ev and Peter groped their way along the hall, toward the light that glowed faintly from under the kitchen door. Stale warmth hit their faces as they opened it. Ches was not surprised to see them.

"Youngsters," he said. "Just made a fresh pot of tea."

The tinned milk Ev poured into her tea was curdled. She drank it anyway, to be polite. Peter left his untouched.

Ches Barrett was not a man to waste words. "I take it," he said, "You remembers what happened to you, Ev maid."

Ev nodded.

"Tell me."

Ev told him the story, just as she had told Peter. "So I want to go back," she finished, "To find that little man and see if I can get the wish. I want to use it to make my father safe."

Ches sat for a long time without speaking. Peter waited impatiently. Tell her, he urged Ches silently. Tell her to give it up.

Then Ches spoke slowly and with care. "He promised you your heart's desire, did he? Well, I'll tell you maid, there's not many knows what their heart's desire might be. You do, and that makes you luckier than most." He fell silent again.

"That's all you got to say!" Peter spoke so loudly that the dishes rattled on the shelf. "Aren't you going to tell her what a risk she's taking? For God's sake, Uncle Ches, have you gone soft in the head?"

Ches looked at him sharply. "Peter, my son, short of tying Ev to the bedpost, how do you propose to stop her?"

Ev spoke up quickly. "Peter was hoping you might be able to tell me something that would help. When to go to the spring house, how to keep safe."

"He was, was he?" Ches asked. He looked at Peter with a faint smile that Peter could not return. "Well, I think you knows as much as I do. More perhaps since I've only ever heard the music and you've seen its maker. Saturday is the new moon. I make that a good time to look, Saturday night. Keep your heart's desire clear in your mind, and that should lead you to him. Keep your silver in your hand. It saved you once. And don't take your eyes off the fellow, if you finds him. They're devilish clever from all I've heard."

"You never heard of any granting no wishes, I guarantee," Peter said. He didn't care how rude he sounded.

Ches looked at him mildly. "No, my son, I never has. Does that mean they couldn't if they tried?"

Peter said nothing.

"I wanted Peter to come with me," Ev told Ches. "He wouldn't say he would." Peter could hear the confidence in her tone. She seemed sure the old man was on her side now.

"Well now, maid, that's something only Peter can decide."

"Yes, I guess that's true," Ev said. They sat together for a while, Peter saying nothing. When they left, Ev touched the old man's shoulder. "Thank you, Uncle Ches," she said.

Peter still could not believe that Ches would encourage Ev to go back to the spring house. Out in the road, he tried to talk to her once more.

"You can't go back there Ev," he said.

"I certainly can."

Might as well talk to the ocean, he thought, but he kept on. "Think of your mother, at least. First your father goes missing, now what if something happens to you?"

"Peter I am thinking of my mother. I'm doing this for her."

"Isn't that what your father said?" Peter asked. His voice was bitter.

They were in front of his door now. The muffled voices of the women in the kitchen carried out to them. Ev turned on him furiously and whispered, "Don't you talk that way about my father. You don't have to come with me if you're so scared. I'll go by myself. Just don't try to stop me."

She rushed for the door, but Peter caught her by the hand. "Don't go in just yet. Let me talk to you. Please don't be angry with me Ev," he said in a low voice. "This is something I've been afraid of for as long as I can recall."

Peter looked at Ev. In this dim light, her eyes seemed as dark and cold as the water in the harbour below. "That's your problem, isn't it?" she said. Her words were like a slap in the face. She pulled her hand from his and went into the house.

They said nothing while waiting for Dr. McCallum. After Ev left, Peter put his jacket on and headed back towards the Barrett house. Ches Barrett had not moved from his chair in the kitchen. "Sit down, Peter, my son," he said. "I knows you're mad at me. Perhaps you got a right to be. But she knows her heart and she got to follow it."

Peter found it difficult to put his feelings into words. After a long time he said, "She could come to harm out there. You knows that as well as I do."

"Yes my son," Ches replied, his voice calm and quiet, "But how would it be to have her wonder for the rest of her life if her father died because she never tried to save him? As long as she thinks she might be able to, this is something she must do."

Now finally Peter understood. But he still could not speak.

"There's something you got to do as well Peter," Ches said after a long minute.

Peter studied his hands and the room filled with a heavy silence. Ev's last, angry words still rang in his ears.

"I know," Peter said at last. "I got to face my fears."

"Perhaps. But something besides."

Finally Peter raised his eyes to look at Ches. "What's that?"

"You knows your heart's desire too. Just as she does. Don't let it slip away from you, my son. If you wants her to stay, you got to tell her so."

"Perhaps I have no right to ask."

"I think you knows you do."

When Peter returned to his own house his Nan was already in bed. He lay awake a long time, looking up to the cliffs above his window before he could finally sleep.

Chapter Fifteen

That night, Ev dreamed she was up on Signal Hill, heading down towards the spring house. Peter was farther up the hill behind her, calling her name. "Ev. Ev."

She sat up in bed almost before she was awake. Someone *was* calling. "Ev, please wake up." It was her mother. The house was dark and quiet. Pulling her tartan bathrobe on against the chilly night, she hurried across the hall. Her mother was sitting up in bed.

"What is it Mum?" she asked.

"Don't be alarmed, Ev, but it's the baby. I need some clean towels, the water's broken. We may need to wake your grandfather up, but just get me some towels for now."

Ev dashed down the stairs to the linen closet. The sunshine-and-fresh-air smell that met her when she opened the door seemed out of place in the middle of this winter's night. She grabbed two thick towels and ran back up the stairs. There was no time to think or worry yet, only to do what needed to be done.

When she returned, her mother was sitting on the edge of her bed. She'd changed her night-gown.

"Are you all right?" Ev asked, handing her the towels.

"Yes, I'm fine," she said, putting the towels on the bed sheets. "I'm waiting for the contractions to start now. The strength of the contractions, how far apart they are, will give me an idea how this labour will go," she explained.

"Are you frightened?" Ev asked.

"Only a little. More excited. The baby's a little early, and that may cause trouble, but I'm ready to do what I need to." She did look excited.

"Do you want me to get Grandpa now?" Ev asked.

"Not yet. We'll let him sleep until the contractions start," her mother said.

They were still waiting when the sun came up three hours later. Ev had watched her mother's excitement turn to impatience, then something like despair. As they heard her grandparents stirring below, she saw a tear trickle down her mother's cheek.

"I'm sorry," she said, wiping it away. "It's just not a very good start. You'd better get your grandfather now."

"Nina," her grandfather said when he entered the bedroom, "You should have called me before this. Don't worry, Ev. I'll bet the potholes on the road to the Grace will get your mother's labour going." Even though he joked, he looked worried. But her mother seemed calmer.

"We never did settle on a boy's name, Ev," she said later when she kissed Ev goodbye. "Think about it for me."

And then they were gone. The oatmeal porridge Millie put before Ev that morning could have been sawdust. She knew her grandmother said something, something about not worrying and excellent medical care, but Ev barely heard her.

The morning was grey and bleak. A cold, damp wind blew in off the ocean as Ev walked to school. Through the Narrows, a lone fishing boat was making its way out of the harbour into the coal-black sea. Ev was almost at school before she remembered her fight with Peter the night before. Well, she thought, Ches is right. I won't ask him to come with me again.

She stopped for a moment, leaning against the wrought iron fence before taking the steps down into the schoolyard. Her father, now her mother and the baby, it was too much to expect anyone to handle alone, even without this crazy idea of finding some little man and asking for a wish.

She thought about running away. I could take the train to Heart's Content and get a ride to Belbin's Cove from there. She closed her eyes and pictured herself running into the house, climbing the stairs and throwing herself onto her bed. She could feel the soft old quilt on her cheek, hear the squeak of the springs. She even remembered the smell of her room with its worn linoleum and the faded wallpaper they always meant to change. I'd be safe there, she thought. But when she opened her eyes she knew that going back to the house in Belbin's Cove now wouldn't change a thing. There isn't any way to get back to the time when Mum and Dad took care of everything for me, she thought.

Peter was waiting for Ev as soon as she entered the school. Ev was afraid he might be angry with her, but he came directly over. "Your grandfather called Nan from the hospital. She must be with your mother by now," he said.

"I was up half the night with my mother, waiting for something to happen." Ev said. "I'm scared." But as she spoke, she realized that she already felt stronger and calmer. It helped to know that Peter wasn't angry at her for being so mean the night before. The bell rang and they went towards the door together.

The morning passed so slowly. Ev couldn't follow her school work at all, but it was better to be here than pacing about at home. Going to the hospital was out of the question, of course. A girl Ev's age would never be allowed near the maternity ward, even if her grandfather was a doctor. At dinnertime, Ev rushed home. Millie met her at the door alone. "Your grandfather called from the hospital about an hour ago. He said you shouldn't worry, that they're doing everything they can."

"Has the labour started?" Ev asked.

Millie frowned. "Not yet," she said. "Your grandfather says they're going to wait a while longer to see if it don't start up on its own. If nothing happens by this evening, they'll do something. That's really all he told me."

Ev looked around. "Where's Grandmother?"

Millie sighed. "She was nervous as a cat. But at least this gives her something to think about. After your grandfather called she said she couldn't stand it any more and she was going to the hospital just to wait. I think she intends to wait in your grandfather's office. I don't imagine she'll bother your mother," Millie added.

"I hope not."

The afternoon passed even more slowly. When school was finally let out, Peter walked home with Ev. As they walked, Ev felt as if she was being tugged in the opposite direction, towards the hospital where her mother was. She was so busy thinking about this that she said nothing.

"Are you still going up on the hill?" Peter asked after a while.

Ev nodded.

"Well, that's one good thing about your mother being in the hospital and all," he said. Ev looked at him as if he must be crazy. What possible good could there be in this? "It will make it easier for you to slip away, you see," he explained. When she said nothing, he added, "Ev, perhaps you'd rather not go now." Ev noticed the hopeful note in his voice.

"You know I'm not going to change my mind, Peter. It's just. . . well, I was thinking I may have to decide who I want to use this wish to save now." She fell silent again and they walked on.

Ev was quiet for a very long time.

"Peter," she said at last, "How. . . how did your mother die? Do you know?"

"I'm not supposed to know, I'm sure, but I listened a couple of times when Nan was talking about it with other women. I wanted to know."

Ev nodded. "Tell me?"

"It wasn't at all like what's happening to your mother, Ev. My mother didn't have much trouble, not for a first child, Nan said. Everything went fine. That's one reason why Nan didn't bother to call a doctor, there was nothing she needed help with."

"So what went wrong?"

"Well, they never knew. A few hours after I was born, she just started to haemorrhage. It was so fast, Nan said, that there was nothing for it. By the time your grandfather got there, she was dead."

"My grandfather. I never knew."

"Well, yes. He signed my birth certificate and my mother's death certificate the same day. I sometimes thinks, well, he seems fond of me, and perhaps that's part of the reason why, that he feels somehow responsible. But Ev," he added, "None of that has anything to do with your mother. Things have changed now. She's in the hospital. They can do more there."

Ev nodded again. If only there was some way to be sure.

When they came to Ev's house, she hurried to the front door, but as soon as she saw Millie's face, she knew nothing had changed.

"Your grandfather said he'd come home with

your Nan for a while, to have supper and let you know what's happening. He said Mrs. Bursey is staying on, so Peter should eat supper here." She turned to Peter. "He wanted to know if you'd be all right alone, out to the Battery. It's likely your Nan will be gone the night."

"She's been gone the night more times that I can count, borning babies," Peter said. "I'm used to it. But I'll stay for supper."

"Good," Millie said. "There's a pot of tea in the kitchen, and you can both give me a hand with supper if you wants."

Ev's grandparents arrived home just as the blackout blinds were being pulled down. Ev's grandfather came straight to her. "People lie to children about childbirth, Ev," he said, "I've never liked that. So I'll tell you all I can. We thought we had something there for a while. But after a few weak contractions the labour stopped." Ev looked down, but he caught her chin in his hand and gently raised it so that she looked at him again. "There's a lot to be hopeful for, Ev. The baby's heartbeat is strong. The danger now is that an infection might set in. We've been watching your mother carefully, and there's no sign of that yet. Now, there's a drug that we can give to start the labour. If nothing has happened by the time I go back this evening, we'll see about that."

"Why didn't you try that before?" Ev asked.

"It's always better to let nature take its course," he said. Then he turned to Peter. "Your grandmother is a rock, Peter. I don't know what we would have done without her. And your mother, Ev, has been strong and calm in spite of everything. I couldn't help thinking how proud Duncan would be."

There didn't seem to be anything more to say.

When Peter sat down at the table beside Ev a short time later, he looked around the dining room, all dark wood and white linen, the china and silver winking in the light from the chandelier. It was a far cry from the old kitchen table where he normally ate. He knew that no one gave his presence here much thought today, but he couldn't help hoping that Ev's grandmother might like him, even though she'd barely glanced at him. She'd seemed to like him well enough when they met before.

Dr. McCallum kept the conversation going. "How is that boat coming along Peter?" he asked.

"Best kind, Doctor McCallum," Peter answered. "I mean fine. We've laid the keel on her now. That's good progress." As he spoke, Millie brought in the plates. Peter noticed that Ev took her napkin from beside her plate and laid it in her lap, then picked up the larger of the two forks. He did the same.

"And how is your school work coming?" Ev's grandfather asked.

"Good. I'm getting a bit ahead in arithmetic now. Miss Smith says I can make a start on some algebra after Christmas. The English and history don't come to me as fast, but I'm working on them."

"I believe we have some old algebra books around here, don't we Gwen? You're welcome to borrow them if you want Peter."

Gwen McCallum stared at her husband. "Ian, those books belonged to Duncan," she said. Then she turned to Peter. "What do you expect to do when you finish school?" It was the first time she'd spoken to him all evening.

"Well, out where I lives, people hardly call it work if you gets to sit down while you're doing it," Peter joked. No one seemed to find that funny. "I'm hoping after I finish high school to find a position with a firm as a clerk," he continued quickly. "A shipping firm would suit me best, but you know, you takes what you gets."

"Yes," Gwen McCallum said. "One does take what one can get."

Peter knew he was being corrected. He felt as if his ears were on fire.

"Oh, I should think you can expect to do a little better than that," Dr. McCallum said. There was something about the way he said it, something cheerful and even a little mysterious that made Peter realize he was thinking of that scholarship.

"I'm sure it's a matter of money," Ev's grandmother said.

"Well, Gwen, there are ways around that," Ian McCallum replied in a quiet voice.

Peter wished himself home, eating supper in the kitchen of his house at the Battery.

After supper, Ev's grandfather offered to drive Peter home, but Peter could see everyone was anxious for Dr. McCallum to return to the hospital so he insisted on taking the streetcar. He wasn't sorry to leave the big house.

Outside, the dark streets were filled with noisy, restless servicemen looking for excitement on a Friday night. The streetcar seemed to take forever but it finally rumbled up.

Sitting in the streetcar, Peter thought about Ev going up Signal Hill alone tomorrow night in the dark and cold. All day he'd waited for her to ask him again, even though he still didn't know what he would say to her. She hadn't asked. He'd never met anyone as stubborn and pigheaded. As fearless and determined. He had to smile.

Then he thought about supper and stopped smiling. That grandmother of Ev's, he thought, what a hard case she is. With someone like her, he knew, he would always be so busy remembering to say "take" and "get" instead of "takes" and "gets" that he'd never be able to think. It was more than that though. Even the dining room in the McCallum house, the linen napkins and more than one fork beside the plate, it all reminded him that he didn't belong in a place like that. He couldn't imagine that he ever would. There might as well be a pane of glass between me and Ev, he thought. I could spend the rest of my life beating against it like a moth against a window and never get inside, only wreck myself trying.

Chapter Sixteen

Peter woke up the next morning with the sound of the telephone in his ears. He stumbled, barefoot, downstairs and into the darkened kitchen to stop the incessant ringing. It was Ev.

"I can only talk for a minute," she said.

"Any word about your Mom?" Peter asked.

"No, not yet. Peter. . ." He could hear her hesitate. "I just want you to know that my grandmother goes to bed at ten. I'm going to sneak out of the house then. I'll be at the bottom of Signal Hill Road around ten-thirty."

Peter stood there, silent, trying to think of something to say.

"Hello?" Ev said finally, "Peter, are you there?" She must have thought the line had gone dead.

"Yes. I'm here."

"Oh. Well, goodbye." And she was gone. That last word sounded final.

When Peter hung up, he lifted the blackout

blinds. It was a fine day, cold but sunny and still. He ate breakfast, trying not to hear that word, goodbye. But it echoed in his ears just the same. After breakfast, he headed over to Ches Barrett's. There was still that skiff to think about.

As soon as Ev put the phone down it rang, like an alarm announcing that she had done something wrong. She jumped. Don't be silly, she told herself, pick it up. On the other end of the line, her grandfather sounded tired.

"Well, labour finally started up in the night, Ev." He didn't sound as pleased as he ought to.

"Is everything okay?"

"It's going slowly. We have to hope for the best, dear. I'll let you know as soon as there's any news."

He talked for a few minutes more without saying much. When Ev hung up she supposed she should feel better, but she didn't. Grandpa sounded so worried.

Please, let them be safe before tonight, she thought. Don't make me have to choose between my father and Mum and the baby. I'll be so good, if only I don't have to choose.

Ev's grandmother came down a few minutes later. There were dark circles under her eyes. "Was that the telephone I heard?" she asked.

"Yes." Ev told her the news as briefly as possible. She didn't want to cause trouble, but after the way her grandmother had treated Peter last night she couldn't feel very friendly, even if she wasn't exactly happy with Peter herself at the moment.

Breakfast was eaten in silence. Then, as she was about to leave the table Ev's grandmother said, "Under the circumstances, I don't suppose you'll be gallivanting off to the Battery today with that friend of yours, will you?"

Ev took a deep breath before replying. "No Grandmother, I won't." I will not get angry with her, she told herself. I will not lose my temper.

"I don't know what your grandfather was thinking of last night," her grandmother said. "Offering Duncan's books to that boy."

"Peter's working hard at school, Grandmother. I think Grandpa only wants to help him get on." Ev dug her nails into the palm of her hand.

"He's a very common boy Evelyn."

The blood rushed to Ev's face and she stood up, almost knocking her chair over. "Grandmother," she said, "You don't know Peter. There isn't anything common about him. He's intelligent and kind-hearted, and. . . and you'd better get used to him, because I have no intention of choosing my friends to please you." Ev shook as she spoke.

Silence fell. How could I make such a fuss with everything else to worry about? Ev thought. She looked down, waiting for the axe to fall. But nothing happened. After a moment she looked up again. Her grandmother was smiling.

"Are you laughing at me?" Ev asked.

"No, I'm not. I'm remembering. When your father brought your mother home to meet us I didn't exactly take to her. Perhaps your parents have told you that story. But Duncan made it clear to me that your mother was going to be part of his life, whether I liked it or not. He used almost the same words you did just now." She paused. "Duncan will never be dead, my dear, as long as you're alive." Ev's grandmother stood up. "I've never been particularly kind to your mother. I know that. I hope. . . I want to have the opportunity to make that up to her. Now, we must save our energy for the important things and try to get along. Perhaps I am too old to change, Ev, but if you try to keep your temper, I'll try to keep my opinions to myself."

Ev was still trying to keep her mouth from falling open when her grandmother left the room.

In spite of the chill in the air, Peter sweated as he chiselled a notch in the keel of the skiff. The work demanded an almost impossible combination of brute strength and delicacy. He loved it. When Peter and Ches lifted the first set of timbers into place, they slid without forcing into the notch Peter had carved and held firm.

After Peter secured the timbers, he and Ches stood back to examine their work.

"Hand and glove, my son," Ches said. It was as close to praise as he'd ever come. Peter looked at the vessel. It was beginning to look like the skeleton of a beached whale. Only it wasn't dead; it was coming to life under their hands.

Ches sat down, taking out his pipe and Peter knew their work was finished for the day. The sun was low in the sky. All day, while he worked, Peter kept glancing up at the workbench, expecting to see Ev there, busy with her knife. It was as if a part of him was missing. How would Ev's mother be getting on, he wondered. And Ev herself? It would still be hours before she could slip away. Fear and excitement rushed back to him as he thought about the spring house on Signal Hill.

"Troubles," Ches said suddenly, "Is like birds. They comes in flocks."

Peter nodded.

"That girl," Ches went on, "Has seen more trouble in these few weeks than some people sees in a lifetime. She's a strong one, though."

Peter hesitated. Until Ev came, they'd never talked openly about the fact that Ches knew things no one else could know. Well, he thought, everything has changed since then. "Uncle Ches," he said at last. "What do you suppose happened to Ev's father?"

Ches waited such a long time before speaking that Peter thought he hadn't heard, or was pretending that he hadn't.

"A child who never sees his father," he finally said, "will often have the power, same as a seventh son. Not always, mind you, but often. Keep that in mind."

Then he rose and went towards his house, leaving Peter puzzle out his words.

Night wrapped itself around Ev like a cold blanket when she stepped outside, blinding her after the bright warmth of the kitchen. Groping for the wooden porch rail, she cautiously felt her way down the steps and along the alley beside the house, moving as quickly as she dared. Her heart raced as she passed under her grandmother's bedroom window. In her hand she held Peter's silver five cent piece.

She reached the street and turned towards the Battery. No lights shone from the windows of houses she passed, of course, but her eyes began to adjust to the darkness. The streets were full of servicemen, as always on Saturday night. Ev huddled into her old coat, shielding herself from the cold, wishing she was invisible. It was later than she'd hoped, and she'd have to hurry to reach the foot of Signal Hill before ten-thirty, just in case Peter was there.

He had to be there, she told herself.

He wouldn't be there.

She walked along Military Road, past the high wrought iron fence of Bannerman Park, the old stone legislature building at the end of the park and beyond it, Government House. As she walked, she thought about her mother. All day she'd waited for news. When darkness finally fell, Ev was so anxious she could hardly sit still. She'd paced the parlour until her grandmother said, "Evelyn, my dear, I know you're worried about your mother, but could you please sit down for a few minutes?"

Just then the phone rang and Ev flew into the hall, pouncing on it.

"Tell your grandmother I won't be home for supper, Ev. I can't leave your mother now," her grandfather had said.

"How is Mum?" Ev asked.

"The labour has been intermittent, on again, off again. But, we should be able to use forceps soon and, God willing, everything should be settled by tomorrow morning." Ev remembered how her heart sank. It wasn't the news she'd wanted to hear. Crossing Military Road, Ev shivered. Just what did Grandpa mean, "everything should be settled?" Why hadn't he said everything would be fine?

When she turned the corner by the Newfoundland Hotel, Ev hesitated. Suddenly the bedroom in her grandparents' house seemed a thousand miles away. What am I doing out here? she thought. I want to go home. She didn't even realize she'd used the word home to mean her grandparents' house. Ev forced herself on. As she turned towards Signal Hill, an icy blast from the open sea caught her. Just a few minutes more and she would be at the foot of Signal Hill Road.

A group of noisy Canadian sailors loomed on the sidewalk ahead. Ev hunched her shoulders down as she passed them. Just when she thought she was safe, one of them grabbed her by the arm.

"Hey, missy, what's your hurry?" he said. He seemed good-natured enough, but Ev could smell the liquor on his breath and he didn't let her go.

"I've got to get home," Ev lied. "Please let me go." She wanted to run away.

"Let her go Andy, she's just a kid," one of the others said.

"Aw, come on, the night's just started," the one called Andy said. "Come to a dance with us, eh? We're just going to a dance. We won't hurt you." He did a few dance steps on the street, still holding her arm.

"No," Ev said, afraid she might start to cry if he wouldn't stop.

Then one of the others took the sailor's hand from her coat. "Let her go, buddy," he said. "Go on kid. Maybe in a few years, if the war lasts that long, eh?" he grinned at her. Ev turned and ran without saying a word, the raucous laughter of the sailors following her down the windy street. The night was beginning to seem like a nightmare.

When she approached the foot of Signal Hill Road, Ev stopped. The streets were empty and she knew it was over. In spite of anything she might have said before, she wasn't brave enough to go up to the spring house alone. A tear brimmed up, hot against the cold night air.

When she felt the hand on her shoulder, she jumped.

"You're some nervous tonight, Ev," Peter laughed.

"Where were you?" Ev cried. The tear trickled down her cheek.

"Steady now. I just stepped between them houses to get out of the wind, is all. Your nerves is shot." He put both his hands on her shoulders to calm her. "Now, I haven't heard from Nan all day. Tell me what's happening."

Ev told him what she knew about her mother.

"I don't want to lose her, Peter," she ended. "I feel as if I just got her back. And I want the baby to be safe. And I want my father to be safe." She sighed. "Remember what Uncle Ches said about keeping m heart's desire clear in my mind?"

Peter nodded.

"Well, when I spoke to him, I knew just what I wanted. Now, I have no idea."

They said nothing for a moment. In the silence there were shouts of laughter, the sound of a bottle breaking somewhere, the noises eerie and out of place in the darkness.

Then Peter spoke. "This is a hard job you set yourself, Ev. I don't wonder you got a case of nerves," he said. Ev was afraid would try to talk her out of going again. Instead he simply said, "We'd best be on our way. You knows how long it takes me to get anywhere."

Ev fell in beside him gratefully. "I didn't think you would come," she said.

"Well, I never thought I would either."

"What changed your mind?"

"I was afraid not to."

She looked at him, puzzled. "Afraid not to?"

He stopped for a moment and looked at her. Then he looked down. "I'm afraid of what we might find up there, Ev. Make no mistake about that. But, I got to thinking this afternoon, and I realized there was only one thing that scared me more."

"What was that?"

"The thought of you going up there alone."

They walked on in silence, past the last of the

houses. Somehow, the sky above the ocean was even blacker than the sky over the city. Before them, the rising mass of Signal Hill was something they could feel more than see. The wind echoed hollowly out over the barrens. Ev strained her ears for music, but there was none. Then it was time to leave the road. Ev hesitated. The road was safe.

Even though Peter was shaking inside his coat, he turned to her when she stopped. "Ev," was all he said. But that made it possible for her to go on. Her heart pounded so hard she could hear very little else. It was so dark. After a few minutes, Peter almost lost his footing and Ev had to steady him. The warm, solid feel of his shoulder calmed her.

They could make out the outline of the spring house now. There was still no music. Ev saw the rock where Peter had sat the day she stumbled out and into his arms. They reached the doorway.

Peter didn't want to look, though whether he was more afraid of what he might see or what he might not, he couldn't have said.

Suddenly Ev sprinted ahead of him, into the spring house. "No," she cried. "Wait!" The last word was pure anguish, echoing out over the darkness.

Peter saw nothing. "What was it?" he asked.

"I'm not sure. There was something. I know there was something. Now it's gone."

She stood there for a long time without moving. It was cold, and Peter wanted to suggest they leave. Then Ev went to the well.

She placed the palm of one hand against the stone covering it. It was cold as death. She felt the cold travel through her hand, up her arm, into her heart. She placed her other hand against the stone, braced her legs against the rough ground and began to push with every ounce of spirit, every ounce of strength. She pushed until the palms of her hands were numb and her fingernails ached. Until her arms felt locked. The stone did not move.

Peter stood frozen. Finally, Ev's arms fell to her sides. The silver coin that she'd held in her hand all that time fell to the ground unnoticed. Peter went to her then. He didn't say anything. He didn't touch her. He just waited.

"I wanted to do the right thing, Peter," Ev said finally. "I wanted to make everything right." She wasn't even crying. She was beyond the point where tears might help.

"You did everything you could, Evelyn. That's as much as any of us can do. Now, let me see you home."

Just as they left the valley, Ev heard something, wild and haunting on the wind. Then it was gone. "Did you hear that?" she turned to Peter.

He looked at her blankly and she knew, even before he spoke, that he hadn't. "What was it?" he asked.

"Probably only the wind," Ev said.

They didn't talk as they walked back to the city. A jeep full of American servicemen passed them going down the road from the military base on Signal Hill, the men shouting into the night. Ev felt empty inside, but somehow lighter too, as if a stone had been lifted from her heart. I didn't want to choose which one to save, she thought. No one should have to make a choice like that.

The war will go on. My father may be dead. I don't know what will happen to my mother and the baby and I can't change a thing. All I can do is live with what I have, whatever that is. What do I have? she thought. Well, Grandpa and Grandmother. They mean more to me now than they did when we came here. She thought about how much she loved her grandfather. Even Grandmother isn't the ogre I thought she was. She almost smiled, remembering what her grandmother had said that morning about trying to make things up to her mother and keeping her opinions about Peter to herself.

And there was Peter.

She glanced over at him now as he walked beside her. It always hurt her to watch him walk because it looked so painful, but he never complained. And here he was, facing a fear he'd carried since childhood, now walking so far on this cold night when he could have been safe in his own home.

Suddenly Ev realized she couldn't go back to Belbin's Cove, not to live. That place belonged to her childhood, a part of her life that was over now. This was where she wanted to be.

It was well after midnight when Peter and Ev arrived at her grandparents' house. "I'd better slip in the back," Ev whispered. "The front door is nearer to Grandmother's room. You don't have to come with me."

"I seen you this far, Ev. I'll see you to the door."

"Well, okay, but we'll have to be quiet."

They slipped along the alley. It was impossible to tell if any lights were on in the house behind the blackout blinds, but Ev imagined Millie would have come home and turned them off by now. On the porch, she turned to face Peter.

"The other night in front of your house when I said, well, that you weren't brave. I was wrong. If you hadn't met me tonight, I wouldn't have been able to go up there alone." Peter only nodded and Ev went on. "I guess I was pretty silly, thinking I could get some magic wish and make everything better. Peter, I don't know what I'd do without you."

"Well, I suppose you'll learn when you gets back to Belbin's Cove, won't you?" Peter said, trying to joke.

"I've thought about that, you know. I'm not so sure I want to go back any more."

He reached out and touched her cheek with the back of his hand. "Ev, I wish you would stay. You knows as much, I think."

Ev nodded. "I'd better go in now," she said. She took out her key and opened the door. When she slipped into the kitchen, the unexpected light blinded her. Then she heard her grandfather's voice.

"Sit down, Evelyn," he said. "I'll tell Peter to come in."

Chapter Seventeen

In the next second, Ev could see. She realized that Mrs. Bursey and her grandmother were sitting at the kitchen table. They both looked grim.

Her grandfather went to the door and called Peter. Ev felt her knees giving way. She sank into a chair. If everyone was here, looking so serious. . .

"My mother..." she said.

"You don't need to worry about your mother, Ev," her grandfather said as he returned with Peter. "We delivered the baby just after eleven. Your mother is exhausted but they're both fine."

Ev let out a long, slow sigh. Thank you, she thought. Thank you.

Her grandfather continued, "I drove Mrs. Bursey home. Peter wasn't there. We thought we might find him here, but then, well, you were gone too." His voice grew stern. "I don't understand how the two of you, under these circumstances. . ."

Ev found her voice. "What we did tonight was foolish. I'm sorry and we'll never do it again, but please Grandpa, you've got to believe me, there wasn't anything wrong in what we did. I. . . I was just so worried about Mum that I needed to get away." Ev knew that she could never tell them the real reason why she and Peter went out. She could hardly believe it herself.

Ian McCallum studied Ev, then Peter. His face relaxed a little.

"Don't ever worry us like that again," he said. Then he smiled. "Now, you have a lively little baby brother. Ten pounds, if you can believe it. That was one reason why your mother had such a battle. A real little fighter though. He struggled his way into the world. Oh, and before I left she asked me to ask you what you want to call him."

Ev didn't know until she'd spoken what she was about to say. "Ian," she said. "Ian Chesley McCallum."

Her grandfather said nothing, but Ev could see how pleased he was.

"That," said her grandmother, "Is a fine name for a child."

That night Ev dreamed that her father came home and there was a huge party, so big that it filled every room in her grandparents' house. Ev went from room to room, looking for her father, but she couldn't find him. Finally, she went into her grandfather's study and there he was, surrounded by friends. Ev pushed past people to be near him. He was standing with a drink in his hand, listening to a story that someone was telling him, an attentive smile on his face. He didn't stop listening, and he didn't turn to look at Ev, but when she came over, he slipped his arm over her shoulders. That was all.

Ev woke in the morning feeling as if she had been with her father. His smile, his laugh, the weight of his arm across her shoulders, things she had almost forgotten about him were with her again in sharp detail. She lay very still, trying to hold the memory that was already fading in the morning light. Oh, if only I could know that I'll see him again, she thought. She reached for the knife under her pillow and cradled it in her hand.

Being the granddaughter of a doctor had some advantages after all. Even though children weren't allowed in the maternity ward, Ev was able to visit her mother that day. She looked very pale and tired, but she smiled when Ev came in.

"Ian Chesley McCallum," she said. "I like the sound of that. But where does the Chesley come from?"

"From Uncle Chesley Barrett," Ev said. "I think you'd like him."

"Well, maybe when I'm recovered from having the little Chesley we can take him out to meet his namesake."

Ev looked puzzled. "You'd call him Chesley?"

"Well, two Ians in one household would be too confusing, don't you think?"

Ev nodded. "Mum, I've been thinking. Going back to Belbin's Cove might not be the right thing for us. There must be plenty of jobs for nurses right here in town."

"You've started to like it here, haven't you?"

Ev nodded again.

"I imagine Peter Tilley has something to do with that, does he?"

Ev said nothing but she felt her cheeks burn.

"Your grandfather told me the two of you were up to something last night." Ev began to speak, but her mother stopped her. "I don't want to know about it. He said he feels certain it was innocent enough, whatever it was. You can have your secrets as long as I feel I can trust you.

"We don't have to decide what we want to do just yet, Ev. It will be at least a year before we can consider moving out on our own anyway. So much could happen in that time. Now, I'm still feeling pretty worn out. Give me a kiss, then your grandfather will take you along to see the baby."

Ev kissed her mother and left the room. Her grandfather was waiting outside the door, and guided her through the maze of antiseptic green halls to the window of the nursery. A nurse smiled at Dr. McCallum, lifted one of the babies and held him to the window, pulling back the blanket so Ev could see him.

He was big and sturdy, but not fat. His head was covered in blond down so fine you could see all the delicate blue veins on his scalp right through it. A kicker, a fighter, Ev thought. I know you already. He stared directly at Ev for a moment with his father's deep blue eyes, then screwed up his little face and let out a wail that

Ev could hear right through the glass. It was a sound she knew she would get used to.

There was a half holiday that week, and Ev went out to the Battery to see Ches Barrett. He was in his store with Peter, hard at work on the skiff. She took a long thin block of maple from her pocket and gave it to him. "It's getting dry now. It has a nice grain, don't you think?"

"It's a fine piece of wood, maid."

"Do you think you could teach me how to make one of these?" Ev asked, reaching for the net needle. The wood was polished smooth by all the hands that had used it over the years. It felt like something worth having.

"Why would you want to make a net needle, Ev maid?" Ches asked her.

"I think it's beautiful," she said. "I know I can learn from making toys, but I still want to make something useful." Then she glanced at Peter who was busy shaping planks that would eventually be needed for the hull of the skiff. Long curls of clean wood flew from the plane in his hand. He was so deep in his work that she was sure he wasn't listening. "Maybe I'd like to give it to a friend of mine for Christmas," she added.

Ches chuckled. "Peter," he called out, "Have a look at that planking outside for me. I wants to make sure we got enough for all nine strakes." When Peter left the store he turned back to Ev "Net needles will be of no use to that one, not where he's going.

"What do you mean?" Ev cried.

"I only mean to say that his life will not be on

the sea," Ches said calmly. Then he took the net needle from her hand and studied it. "Well, it'll take some time, but I think you're up to making one of these," Ches said.

"I thought you said it would be useless to him," Ev said.

"If you makes it for him, maid, I'm sure it will knit more than nets."

Peter returned carrying an armload of lumber and Ches went to him. Ev watched for a while as they worked on the boat. The things they did were beginning to make sense to her now, as if boat building was a language she could believe she would one day understand. When they were finished, they sat together while Ches smoked his pipe. Ev felt it was the right time to ask the question that had been troubling her since the night on Signal Hill. "Uncle Ches," she said, "I wonder why this happened. The magic being there, and then not being there I mean."

"Well, Ev my maid, 'tis more than I can say," Ches said. Ev remained silent until he went on. "'Tis not the same for everyone, you see. Sometimes, you looks and you know it was a kind of punishment, say when a tiny child is left alone. The parents come back and they find their own child taken and this wizened, sickly creature in its crib. That's for punishment. Then sometimes when people are led astray, maybe that's done just out of spite. But it isn't always so. I remembers once, oh thirty years ago it would have been, a little girl went berry picking out on the barrens on Signal Hill with her family and she vanished without a trace. We must have covered every inch of Signal Hill twice over in the next two days. Not of sign of her. Then, on the morning of the third day, we found her, sitting on a rock, singing, with a dipper full of berries in her hand. Not hungry, not cold, no worse for wear at all. She couldn't tell us where she'd been. And she's alive today, as sane as you or me.

"With you, Ev, I gets the same feeling. It seems to me no harm was meant. Perhaps it didn't happen so's you could gain your heart's desire at all. Perhaps it was meant to save you from some danger we mightn't know of, might never know. There's no way of telling, but I knows this much, it wasn't for no reason at all. If I've learned anything about this sort of thing, I've learned that it's never for nothing."

Ev nodded, but she wasn't convinced. Later, while they waited for her grandfather's car, Ev said, "Peter, Uncle Ches must be wrong. The magic didn't change anything, did it? And now it's gone. Perhaps it was for nothing after all."

"Well, Ches isn't often wrong about these things. Perhaps it's as he said. There might have been some danger we will never even know of. You've been through so much these last few weeks. Some day, I wants you to tell me everything that happened to you, day by day, and then perhaps we'll make some sense of it."

"There's Grandpa now," Ev said, waving to the car as it appeared. She turned to Peter. "All right," she promised, "Someday we will."

It seemed to Ev that her grandmother went a little crazy before Ev's mother and the baby came home on Saturday. The white bassinet that had once held Ev's father lay waiting in the parlour, with soft, lacy coverlets of white wool spilling out of it. Every five minutes, her grandmother made some small adjustment to it, or asked Ev if she thought the house was warm enough. Ev sat in the parlour, trying to be tolerant, with her father's copy of *A Midsummer-Night's Dream* in her lap. Even with her grandmother's interruptions, she finally managed to reach the last page. She sat with the open book in her lap. What had happened in the spring house seemed like a dream as well. Maybe, Ev thought, that's the best way to remember it. Unless Peter is right, and I don't see how he can be. What possible danger could I have been in?

"Evelyn, dear, don't you feel a draft from the fireplace?"

"No Grandmother, I'm sure I don't." Ev slammed the book shut harder than she intended to. I bet she never fussed like this for me, she thought. Just because little Chesley is a boy. But, before she could say anything, Millie burst in from the kitchen.

"The car's here," she cried. "They're coming up the back steps now."

When Ev's mother was settled in an arm chair and the sleeping Chesley was safely stowed in his royal bassinet, Ev's grandmother smiled mysteriously. "I have a present for someone," she said and she disappeared.

More baby stuff, Ev thought. Over the past week the house had filled up with more baby gear than she would have thought possible. Such a fuss over a little baby. Her grandmother entered again with a large, flat box from Ayre's. But Ev was more than a little surprised when the box was put into her aims.

"Open it," her grandmother demanded.

She must think Mum's too tired, Ev thought.

But inside the box was a new winter coat, Ev's size. She ran her hand over the thick wool cloth, a beautiful warm red. She stood and tried it on. It fitted tight to her waist, then flared out into a full skirt. It felt like a hug.

"Not black," her grandmother said. "I remembered."

Ev's grandfather looked at her, puzzled. "But red, Gwen? Aren't you worried what people might say?"

"If you spend your life worrying about what other people might say, Ian, you'll have no life at all," Ev's grandmother replied.

Then, before Ev could think to say anything, her mother spoke. "Thank you, Mother," she said. "I think it's lovely."

"So do I," said Ev.

Historical Note

Signal Hill is now a national historic park that welcomes thousands of visitors every year, but the spring house on the barrens exists only in my imagination. The brick band shell in Bannerman Park is, however, very real. My daughter often plays in and around it. None of the six houses beside the park on Military Road resembles the house Ev and her mother shared with Ev's grandparents. That house is a product of my imagination as well. The hydro dam at the place I've called Belbin's Cove in this book was not actually built until 1957. I moved its construction ahead some years to give Ev's family an excuse to live in a place I love.

By 1942, midwives like Mrs. Bursey worked mainly among the poor of St. John's, or with women who had relied upon them for years. Younger women and those who were not poor regarded the hospital as the best place to have their babies, just as Ev's mother did. Midwives could, and did, work as private maternity nurses in hospitals and women's homes and were still active outside of St. John's, assisting at births well into the 1960s in many parts of the province. Doctors in Newfoundland generally got along well with midwives and many, like Dr. McCallum, worked closely with them.

The blackout continued in St. John's from 1942 until the war ended in 1945. Newfoundland became part of Canada in 1949, but that's another story.

Acknowledgements

This book owes a great deal to many people. The women who talked to me about midwifery and childbirth during research for my doctorate in folklore helped to shape Mrs. Bursey and Dr. McCallum in my mind, allowing me to understand how they might have worked together. Otto and Elsie Wells shared their memories of the Battery one very wet December morning. Barbara Rieti's *Strange Terrain: The Fairy World in Newfoundland* and David Taylor's *Boat Building in Winterton, Trinity Bay, Newfoundland* added important details to this story. Philip Hiscock of Memorial University of Newfoundland's Folklore and Language Archive directed me to other valuable research, gave advice on the finer points of Newfoundland speech and always believed in my ability to tell this story. Gary Smith found a net needle in Gooseberry Cove.

The Writers' Alliance of Newfoundland and Labrador enabled me to meet members of St. John's lively writing community. Gail Collins, Kevin Major, and Georgina Queller read all or part of this book. Members of the Newfoundland Writers' Guild listened patiently to chapter after chapter of the work in progress. Helen Porter, who is the same age as Ev and attended the same school, helped me approach an understanding of this time and place. Gerry Rubia, who edited the final manuscript, gave the book a title. She also provided many practical details of coping with a physical handicap which shaped Peter. Bernice

Morgan must be thanked for her gentle criticisms, and for helping me to understand the growing pains that beset a novelist. Without the support and encouragement of these and other Newfoundland writers, and the Alliance itself, this book would not exist.

I would like to thank Don Morgan for not sending me a letter of rejection, for his careful attention to detail and his kindly good nature.

And finally, Leona Trainer, for taking a second look.